Witch Is When The Floodgates Opened

Published by Implode Publishing Ltd
© Implode Publishing Ltd 2016

The right of Adele Abbott to be identified as the Author of the Work has been asserted by her in accordance with the Copyright, Designs and Patents Act 1988.

All rights reserved, worldwide.
No part of this publication may be reproduced, stored in a retrieval system, or transmitted, in any form or by any means without the prior written permission of the copyright owner.

The characters and events in this book are fictitious. Any similarity to real persons, dead or alive, is purely coincidental and not intended by the author.

Chapter 1

The wart on the end of Grandma's nose looked as though it might explode at any moment.

"She said what?" Grandma shouted.

"That she would like to take on responsibility for my tuition as a witch."

"And what exactly did *you* say?"

"I said no, of course. I said you were teaching me, and I didn't need anyone else's help."

"That woman has only been back in Candlefield for five minutes, and already she's wreaking havoc."

Grandma was upset because her arch rival, Martha Chivers, known to everyone as 'Ma Chivers', had approached me, and offered to oversee my development as a witch. Obviously, I'd declined her offer because even though Grandma would never be my favourite person, I'd take her over Ma Chivers any day of the week. And, I never thought I'd say this, but Grandma was actually easier on the eye, and not so mean spirited. Hard to believe, I know.

"So, she just marched in here, did she?" Grandma was still breathing fire.

"Yes, I'd no idea she was coming. She just turned up out of the blue."

"Right. Well, we'll see about that. If she contacts you again, you are to call me immediately. Got it?"

"Got it."

"Good."

With that, Grandma disappeared.

Winky, who'd hidden under the leather sofa the moment Grandma arrived, now crawled back out and gave me a one-eyed look.

"She wasn't very happy, was she?" he said.

"What gave it away?"

"I took cover in case that wart of hers exploded."

"I don't blame you."

"So, who rattled her cage?" he said, scratching an ear.

"She's upset that someone is trying to poach me. It's so difficult being a superstar witch with everyone wanting a piece of you."

"No, seriously." He laughed. "What's really the matter with her?"

"It's true! Grandma is upset because another level six witch wants to take me under her wing."

"If your grandmother had any sense, she'd be glad to get shut of you. I bet you're a nightmare to teach."

"Thanks."

"Anyway, enough of this *witch* nonsense, and on to more important matters. I'm starving."

Winky wasn't exactly thrilled about the cat food I put out for him, but I couldn't afford to buy him salmon all the time. When he'd finished eating, he turned to me, and said, "You haven't forgotten about the darts tournament, have you?"

He'd mentioned this some time ago, but I hadn't been sure if he was serious or not. I knew he played darts; he'd hustled me for ten pounds. Even so, I couldn't convince myself there were darts tournaments for cats.

"Well? Do you remember?" he said, impatiently.

"Yeah, vaguely."

"It's the day after tomorrow. I'll need you to take me and Bella."

"What about Cindy?"

"I'd like to take them both, but that might be a bit—err—awkward."

"Could that be because they don't know about one other?"

"That might have something to do with it. I'd promised Bella that she could watch me play before I met Cindy."

"What's it worth not to mention Cindy to Bella?"

"About the same as for me not to tell Jack about Drake. Or Luther. Or—"

"Okay, okay. I get the idea. I won't say anything."

***

It was nine-thirty, and Mrs V still wasn't at her desk—very unusual. I'd assumed that her bus must have been delayed, but even if it had, she should still have been in by now.

"Hey, Winky."

"I'm busy." He was doing something with his smartphone. He was never off the thing: FelineSocial, Angry Birds. Who knew what else he was looking at on there?

"I just wondered if you'd seen Mrs V this morning?"

"The old bag lady? Yeah, she was in earlier; before you arrived. She put a note on your desk."

"I haven't seen it."

"I took it under the sofa to read."

"Where is it now?"

"Still under there, I assume."

"Would you mind getting it?"

"I'm busy. I've got ten 'licks' now."

"I don't care how many 'licks' you've got. What gives you the right to read my messages?"

"I thought it might have been important. I was going to let you know if there was something which needed urgent attention."

"And how exactly would you have done that?"

"I'd have called you, of course."

"You don't have my number."

"Yeah. Okay, if that's what you want to believe."

"So, are you going to get it for me or not?"

"Nah."

I scrambled under the sofa, and came out covered in dust and cat hair. The message read:

'Jill, sorry to drop this on you at the last minute, but G says she's coming over, and I simply can't face her. Would you tell her that I've emigrated, or fallen down a hole? I'll be back as soon as she's gone. Sorry to leave you in the lurch, Annabel V.'

I couldn't say I blamed Mrs V. Her sister was a nasty piece of work who was always putting her down. I'd just have to get rid of 'G' when she arrived.

My phone rang; it was the twins. They sounded even more excited than usual.

"Jill, you have to come over," Amber said. "We have something we want to show you."

"What?

"You have to come over here," Pearl insisted. "It'll be

much better if you see it."

"I *am* quite busy. I *do* have a business to run you know."

"Yeah, but it's not like you ever have any work, is it?" Amber said.

"Gee thanks!"

"Come over, Jill. It'll be worth it, we promise."

"Okay, I'm on my way."

***

"What do you think?" Pearl said. "It's good, isn't it? It's a chocolate fountain."

"It's very big." I craned my neck to try to see the top of it. "I've never seen one as big as that."

"It was on special offer," she said. "The man said that the small ones are ten-a-penny. This one is the 'Supreme'."

"This man? Was he selling anything else? Snakes? Oil?"

"You're such a cynic, Jill."

Moi?

"It takes up rather a lot of room on the counter doesn't it?" I said. "How will you be able to see the customers?"

"There's still a bit of space at the side. Look." Amber went around the back of the counter, and poked her head through the gap to prove her point.

"Hmm, okay. So how does it work?"

"We haven't figured that out yet," Amber said. "But once it's working, the chocolate will cascade down these levels."

"How many levels are there?"

"On the standard model there are only three, but on the Supreme there are ten. We've got far more levels than anyone else."

"That's great—I guess."

"We'll be able to dip marshmallows, fruit and all sorts of things into it. It'll be brilliant won't it, Jill?"

"Fantastic."

Pearl and I left Amber tinkering around with the fountain.

"Has Aunt Lucy seen it?"

"Don't talk to me about Mum."

"Why, what's happened?"

"Amber and me aren't talking to her."

"Why not?"

"Because she made birthday cakes for Miles Best. She's a traitor!"

I hadn't realised the twins had found out about that. Aunt Lucy hadn't done it deliberately—she'd been making them for a middleman, and had no idea they would be sold in Best Cakes. Once she found out, she stopped supplying them.

"I'm sure she wouldn't have done it if she'd known who they were for."

"Huh! That's what she said, but we think she knew all along. So, we're not talking to her until she apologises."

***

There was still no sign of Mrs V or her sister by the time I called it a day at the office. Maybe G had changed her mind about the visit?

Back at the flat, I decided to have an early night. I was sitting up in bed, reading, when I heard something. It sounded like there was someone in the flat. I grabbed

Dad's old golf club which I always kept under the bed, and crept quietly out of the bedroom. There was someone in the kitchen; I could hear them moving around. Whoever it was, would regret sneaking into *my* flat. I walked on tip toe into the kitchen.

"Mum! What are you doing here?"

"I was just—err. I wanted to—err. To make sure you weren't upset after Ma Chivers' visit."

"Err—no. She's a bit scary, but I'm not *upset*. Do you realise what time it is?"

"Sorry. It *is* rather late isn't it. I wasn't thinking. So, you're okay then?"

"Yeah, I'm fine. I don't think Grandma is though. She was really annoyed when I told her."

"That doesn't surprise me. She and Ma Chivers don't get along at the best of times. Anyway, I suppose I'd better get going. I'm sorry I disturbed you. Goodnight then, dear."

With that, she disappeared. What was that all about? Why was she sneaking around in my kitchen late at night?

Something weird was going on.

Chapter 2

The next morning, there was someone sitting at Mrs V's desk. It *wasn't* Mrs V.

"Good morning, Mrs G."

"Morning, Jill. Annabel seems to have disappeared. I tried her house, but she wasn't there. I assumed she'd be here, but there's no sign of her. I thought you might know where she is?"

"No, sorry, but I'll tell her you called."

"No need. I can see that V has left you in the lurch, so I'm more than happy to help out."

"That really isn't necessary—"

"It's no problem. I'm quite an accomplished PA. Somewhat better than V, if I do say so myself. Is there anything you'd like me to get started on?"

"Not really."

"Well then, perhaps you could make me a cup of tea?"

"*Me* make *you* a cup of tea?"

"Yes please. Milk, no sugar. And do you happen to have any biscuits?"

***

Winky rolled his eye.

"I see we've got the other bookend here again."

"Yeah, it looks like it." I sighed. "I wish I knew where Mrs V has gone."

"I've told you before: it's about time you got rid of the old bag lady, and her sister, and recruited a pretty young thing. Someone who'll show me the kind of love and respect I deserve."

"Don't *I* do that?"

"Only when I'm blackmailing you."

The intercom startled me. Mrs V was so hard of hearing, she never used it. When Mrs G's voice came booming through, both Winky and I almost jumped out of our seats.

"Jill!" Mrs G shouted. "Jill!"

"Yes, Mrs G, I can hear you."

"There's a gentleman out here—a Colonel Briggs. Shall I get rid of him?"

"No, don't do that. Please send him in."

"Alright then—if you're sure."

"Yes. Please send him through."

"Good morning, Jill," the colonel said.

He looked as debonair as ever.

"And good morning to you, young man." He addressed Winky.

Winky eyed him suspiciously. He wasn't a fan of the colonel who ran a charity for dogs.

"What can I do for you, Colonel?"

"I have a friend by the name of Cuthbert Cutts. Actually, *Sir* Cuthbert Cutts. You may have heard of him?"

"No, I don't think so."

"He owns the large stately home on the eastern fringes of Washbridge. He and I were talking at the club the other day, after a round of golf. He's been having a spot of bother, so I mentioned that I knew a good P.I. who might be able to help, and he seemed very keen."

"What's the problem exactly?"

"It's rather delicate. He has a fabulous collection of

antiques, and it seems that one of them has gone missing."

"Was there a break-in?"

"I'm not sure. I thought it best for you to meet with him. Would you have the time, or are you too busy?"

"Well—I am rather busy," I lied. "But as it's you, Colonel, I'm sure I could fit it in."

"Jolly good! Here's his card—perhaps you would give him a call, and arrange a meeting?"

"Certainly. It will be my pleasure."

"Thank you very much. You must come up to the house for drinks some time, Jill. Bring your sister, and Peter, and your young man—if you have one."

Did I have one? It was a good question.

***

As I made my way up Kathy's drive, I noticed they appeared to have a new next door neighbour in the house where I'd got rid of the werewolf.

"Auntie Jill, they've got chickens," Lizzy shouted.

"Lots of them," Mikey said.

"Who has?"

"Let Auntie Jill get in," Kathy said, shooing the kids away from the door. "Come on. It's nearly time for school. Go and get ready."

"We want to show Auntie Jill the chickens," Lizzie said. "Please, can we?"

Kathy sighed. "Okay, but you'll have to be quick."

She disappeared into the kitchen, and I followed the kids upstairs into Lizzie's bedroom which overlooked the neighbour's garden.

"Look, Auntie Jill. Look! Chickens!" Mikey pointed.

I looked down into the neighbour's garden. What I'd thought was a large shed was actually a chicken coop. The back garden was full of chickens. Lots of them.

"Aren't they great?" Lizzie screamed.

"Mum doesn't like them," Mikey said. "But I think they're fantastic."

"Yeah," Lizzie said. "They chase each other around, and they go in and out of their house."

"How long have they been here?"

"Kids, come on. It's time for school," Kathy shouted from downstairs. "Your dad's waiting for you."

"Aw, Mum," Mikey groaned.

"Can't we just watch for a bit longer?" Lizzie pleaded.

"No, it's time to go. Come on, you'll be late."

The kids grabbed their backpacks, and went reluctantly downstairs where Peter was waiting for them.

"Morning, Peter," I shouted from the landing.

"Morning, Jill. I take it the kids have shown you our new neighbours."

"The chickens, you mean?"

"Yeah, just what we needed. I'd better get the kids to school. I'll catch up with you later."

After the kids had left, I caught up with Kathy in the kitchen.

"Don't talk to me about chickens!" she said. "The kids are driving me crackers with them."

"Are you even allowed to keep chickens on this estate?"

"Apparently, yes. I wasn't sure, but Pete checked the bylaws and the leases. It seems there's nothing to stop anyone keeping chickens. And that's not all. They've got a goat out there as well."

"I didn't see it."

"It's tied up on the other side of the garden, thank goodness. But the chickens roam free around the garden."

"Have you actually met your new neighbours yet?"

"Yeah. Frank and Fiona Flood. They're very nice. Middle aged, a little bit hippy, I suppose, which probably explains the chickens. Apparently, they plan to live off the land; they've already started planting vegetables. They're perfectly nice people, there's nothing to dislike about them, except for the chickens. And the goat."

"Have you said anything to them about the livestock situation?"

"I was about to, but then they handed me a box of eggs, and said we could have as many as we liked, as often as we liked. What could I say — other than thank you?"

"Oh well, at least they're not as noisy as your last neighbour."

"That's true. We don't get the awful howling that we had with him. That was all a bit strange. He just disappeared overnight."

"Really?" I feigned surprise. "How strange."

"Why do you buy this rag?" I shouted to Kathy who was in the kitchen, making a cup of tea.

The Bugle loved its dramatic headlines. Today's was 'Double Trouble at Museum'. Another nonsense story — it seemed to be their speciality.

"Pete likes to get it for the sports." She brought through the tea and biscuits.

"Hasn't he heard of the Internet?"

"You know Pete. He's strictly old school."

"There's only one left." I held up the Tupperware box.

"Sorry, I forgot to buy some." Kathy shrugged. "Is that

the only reason you came around here? To eat my custard creams?"

It was actually.

"Of course not! I came to see you, and to see how the kids and Peter were. But a few custard creams would have been nice."

"Anyway, I'm glad you came over. It's saved me having to ring you. I wanted to remind you about the children's party."

This sounded like bad news. "What children's party?"

"I told you about it two or three weeks ago."

Typical Kathy—she did this to me every time. She made out that she'd told me about something when in fact it was the first I'd heard of it.

"I don't remember anything about a children's party."

"You went to it last year. It's the one held at the community centre for the local kids. Don't you remember—you spent most of the time in the toilet hiding from the clown?"

"I was *not* hiding from the clown. I had an iffy tummy, that's all."

"That's strange because, if I remember correctly, your *iffy tummy* only came on when the clown appeared."

"Pure coincidence." I hate clowns—they're evil; all of them.

"Anyway, you'll be pleased to hear that there won't be a clown at this year's party. They're having a Punch and Judy show instead."

"When is it anyway? I might not be able to make it."

"I've already put your name down to help out, so you have to go."

"You never asked if I wanted to help."

"I knew you would." She smirked. "You and I will be helping out with the food and the games."

"How are the kids anyway? Apart from the chicken mania?"

"Oh, you know. Mikey is still playing his drum twenty-four seven." She gave me a look.

"Hey, don't blame me. I didn't buy it; that was Courtney's mum."

"He's driving us insane."

"Can't you *lose* it accidentally on purpose?"

"Oh yeah, and that wouldn't cause a problem."

"You could say someone stole it."

"You really don't know anything about kids, do you, Jill?"

"I know I wouldn't let *my* kids make these things." I held up one of Lizzie's latest beanie creations. She and Kathy were tearing apart my treasured beanie collection, one at a time, then turning them into frankensteinesque creatures. I glanced around the living room. They were everywhere; it was like some sort of freak show.

"I like them," Kathy said.

"You would. You're weird."

***

Grandma's tea room was now open for business. Under highly suspicious circumstances, she'd taken over the shop next door to Ever A Wool Moment. The previous tenant, Rod's Rods, the largest fishing tackle shop in Washbridge, had encountered all manner of unusual problems, ranging from flooding to an infestation of rats. I was convinced that Grandma had been behind it, and that she'd deliberately driven him out, so she could expand her empire.

Kathy worked at 'Ever'. Since starting there, she seemed to have been promoted and given more responsibility almost every week. When I arrived, she was busy behind the counter. When she spotted me, she asked one of the assistants to take over.

"What's this?" I said, pointing to a poster on the wall.

"It's another of your grandmother's sales initiatives."

"Does she ever stop with them?"

"There's no sign of it happening yet."

"What's this one all about?"

"*This* is 'Ever' membership."

"What's that when it's at home?"

"Customers can sign up to become 'members' of Ever A Wool Moment in order to enjoy a number of perks. They get an Everlasting Wool subscription, a pair of One-Size Knitting Needles, and are also entitled to Auto-Refill Coffee."

"Auto-Refill Coffee? How does that work?"

"I don't actually know. Every new member is given a special coffee cup to use in the Ever A Wool Moment tea room. As soon as it becomes empty, it refills itself."

"How is that possible?"

"Don't ask me. Ask your grandmother; it's one of her innovations."

Once again, this sounded suspiciously like magic. The woman was shameless. The rules for living in the human world stated that you should not let humans know that you had magical powers. Grandma continuously flaunted the rules. Why wasn't anyone asking questions? Why wasn't an investigative journalist knocking on her door?

Maybe I should tip off the Bugle, but then I hated the local rag even more than I disliked Grandma.

"How's the tea room doing?"

"Really well. See for yourself."

I glanced inside, and, sure enough, most of the tables were taken. The place was full of women chatting, knitting and drinking from their Auto-Refill cups.

"Some of these old biddies stay in here all day," Kathy said. "They arrive first thing in the morning, and don't leave until we close. The strange thing is that more and more people keep coming in, but the tea room doesn't seem to get any fuller."

"How is that possible?"

Kathy shrugged.

"Where is Grandma anyway?"

"I don't know. She isn't in yet. Not that I'm complaining." Kathy grinned. "I like it better when I'm running the show by myself."

"Has there been much interest in this new membership scheme?"

"Are you kidding? Everyone wants to sign up. We can't keep pace with it."

Surely Grandma couldn't keep getting away with this? She was pushing her luck way too far. Sooner or later, someone would realise that something very suspicious was happening at Ever A Wool Moment.

Chapter 3

I was so busy daydreaming that I totally forgot to be on the lookout for my movie buff neighbour, Mr Ivers, who I normally tried to avoid like the plague.

"Jill, I have some really exciting news."

I doubted that.

"You know I'm now writing a movie review column for The Bugle?"

"Yes, I think you did mention it." A thousand times.

"Well, you'll never guess what happened."

The circulation of the paper has halved?

"I've been invited to attend the London premiere of the new 'Full Force' movie."

"Really? That sounds very exciting." Not.

"It's a great honour, and even better, I can take someone with me."

"That's nice."

"I was wondering if you would like to accompany me?"

"Sorry, I'm busy that day."

"I haven't told you when it is yet."

Whoops! "I have so much work on at the moment—I'm busy every day for the foreseeable future."

"How disappointing. I thought you'd enjoy a trip to the capital. We could have gone on to a club afterwards, and let our hair down."

"That would have been great, but what can I do? Why don't you ask Betty? I believe she's split up from her boyfriend, so she'd probably—"

"I'm not going with *her*. She's so boring. All she ever talks about is sea shells."

"Oh well, got to dash. See you later. Bye."

Phew! Dodged that bullet.

***

The colonel hadn't been exaggerating when he'd said Sir Cuthbert Cutts lived in a 'stately home'. Access was via a long, winding driveway from which I could see the house in the distance. I'd driven past the estate many times, but I'd never actually visited the house, which was currently closed to the general public. A butler answered the door. He was tall and thin, with hair which looked as though it had been slicked back with lard.

"Good morning, madam."

"Morning. I'm Jill Gooder. Sir Cuthbert is expecting me."

"Please follow me."

He led the way into an enormous entrance hall. The sound of my heels on the wooden floor echoed around the vast expanse of the room.

"This way, madam. Sir Cuthbert is in the Long Room."

I followed him up a rather grand staircase. He pushed open a huge, ornate door, and announced my arrival.

"Ah, good morning, young lady." Sir Cuthbert was a very short man: five-one at the most. Apparently, no one had told his tailor because his trousers were two inches too long.

"Good morning, Sir Cuthbert."

"Thank you for coming today, Jill. Colonel Briggs speaks very highly of you. I'm delighted that you were able to take on this case."

"I don't actually know what *the case* is yet."

"Come and sit with me." He gestured to the leather

armchairs which were either side of a huge fireplace. "Can I get you a drink?"

"I wouldn't say no to a cup of coffee."

"Would you like a biscuit with it?"

"I don't suppose you have any custard creams?"

"Actually, we do. I'm rather partial to them myself." He rang a bell, and within moments the butler came back into the room.

"Bertram, would you organise some coffee and biscuits for us, please?"

"Very good, sir."

I quite liked the idea of having a butler. Maybe I should get one? I'd call him Hargreaves.

"So, Sir Cuthbert—" I said. "What exactly is it I can help you with? The colonel said something about an antique going missing?"

"Yes, terrible affair. You probably saw some of the pieces as you came up the stairs. We have a fine collection which has been in the family for generations. One of our most treasured pieces, a vase, has disappeared."

"Was there a break-in?"

"No. There's no sign of one. The damn thing just disappeared. It was there when I went to bed, and the next morning it had gone."

"Have you notified the police?"

Before he could answer, the door opened, and in walked Bertram carrying a tray. He poured the coffee, and held out a plate of custard creams. It seemed that Sir Cuthbert really did have class.

I took two biscuits, somehow resisting the temptation to take more.

"It's nice to meet someone who shares my love of custard creams," Sir Cuthbert said. "They truly are the king of biscuits."

I was warming to this man.

"Ah, there you are, Cuthbert," a female voice came from behind me.

Both Sir Cuthbert and I stood up.

"Jill, this is my wife, Lady Phoebe. Phoebe, this is the young lady I was telling you about."

Lady Phoebe didn't look happy to see me. "So, you're the private investigator woman?"

I nodded.

"Hmm, isn't that rather an unsuitable job for a woman?"

"Phoebe!" Sir Cuthbert said. "Jill comes highly recommended by Colonel Briggs."

"I wouldn't trust anything the colonel has to say. Still you're here now, so I suppose you'll have to do."

"I was just asking your husband what exactly had happened to the vase."

"If we knew that, we wouldn't need you, would we, dear?"

"Have you informed the police?"

"Of course, but do you really think they have enough resources to trouble themselves with this?" Lady Phoebe said. "I doubt we'll hear from them again."

"How much is the vase worth?"

"Somewhere in the region of twelve thousand pounds—give or take a thousand. But to us, it's priceless—simply irreplaceable."

After a while, Lady Phoebe left us to it. Sir Cuthbert

gave me a list of his employees, past and present, but went out of his way to emphasise that he had no reason to suspect that any one of them was responsible for the disappearance of the vase. I told him I would get started immediately.

"Do you have a photo of the vase?" I asked.

"I do indeed," Sir Cuthbert said, taking one from the inside pocket of his jacket. "There you are."

The photo had obviously been taken in the grand entrance hall. The vase, which was front and centre, was much smaller than I'd imagined. If I'd had to describe it in one word it would have been 'ugly'.

"A beauty, isn't it?" Sir Cuthbert beamed with obvious pride.

"Err—yes. It's very—err—small."

"The best things come in small packages."

"Can I keep this photograph?"

"Yes, of course."

***

So, *this* was what my life had come to. I was now chauffeur to my cat.

"Hurry up!" Winky snapped. "Bella will be waiting for us. I told her we'd pick her up at five o'clock."

"I'm *so* sorry, Sir. I didn't realise we were running to such a tight schedule."

"I don't appreciate the attitude. You should be honoured that I'm allowing you to take me. I could have booked a taxi, but I knew you'd want to accompany us to such a prestigious event."

"It's only a darts tournament. Not much prestige going

on there."

"Hold on to this." He handed me a small, red packet.

"What is it?"

"Those are my darts. You can look after them until we get there."

"Thank you very much. You're so kind."

"Just be careful with them—they're precision instruments. I can't use just any old darts, you know."

"I'll guard them with my life."

Bella was waiting outside the apartment block where she lived. I pulled up, opened the rear door, and she jumped in.

"Hello, Bella," I said.

She smiled enigmatically, but didn't speak. I was, after all, only the hired help, and she was a supermodel. I thought I might amuse myself by listening to their conversation, but they spoke in hushed voices, so I couldn't hear what they were saying.

The tournament was being held at a hotel about forty miles west of Washbridge. There were huge banners outside advertising the event. Once I'd parked, I started to walk towards the main entrance.

"Where do you think you're going?" Winky shouted.

"Over there—to the main entrance."

"That's not where we should be headed."

"But it says, 'Open Darts Championship'."

"That's the human event. We're here for the feline event."

"Where's that?"

"Around the back; in the basement."

Winky led the way around the building with Bella by his side. I followed behind, carrying his darts. We reached the entrance where two rough-looking tabby cats stood guard. Winky nodded to them, and they nodded back, both of them eyeing Bella jealously. Winky and Bella started down the steps, and I began to follow when one of the tabbies blocked my way.

"I'm sorry. Where do you think you're going?"

"I'm with him."

"This is a feline only event. No non-felines allowed."

"But I—err—Winky!" I called out.

"Oh yes, of course." He came running back up the steps. I assumed he was going to have a word with the door cats, to persuade them to let me in. Instead, he grabbed the darts and said, "We'll see you later."

With that, he and Bella disappeared inside.

"What about me?" I called, but he'd gone. I turned to the door cat. "Is there no way I can be allowed in?"

"Sorry, no can do." The tabby stood his ground.

"How long will the tournament last?"

"It's usually three or four hours. It'll probably be over around ten thirty."

"What am I meant to do until then?"

"Do I look as though I care?"

He didn't.

Great! So, I'd driven all the way there, and now they'd abandoned me. What was I meant to do for the rest of the evening? I had a good mind to leave them there, and let them find their own way home. But, I knew that would only come back to haunt me. Winky would make my life a misery. Instead, I walked around to the front of the building, and went in through the main entrance. I couldn't have any alcohol because I would be driving, but at least I could quench my thirst. I bought orangeade and a packet of crisps, and made my way through to the main hall. I'd never been to a darts tournament before, and I had no idea what to expect. The hall was packed; most of the audience were in fancy dress.

"Hello there, sexy."

I turned around to see a man dressed in a gorilla costume. He removed the mask. I wished he hadn't—he'd looked better with it on.

"Can I buy you a drink?" he slurred.

"That's okay. I've got one, thanks."

"That's not a drink! You need something stronger. Why don't you have a beer?"

"No, I'm okay, thanks."

"You look lonely. Why don't you come and sit with me? We'll have a great time."

Oh dear.

I cast the 'forget' spell, and beat a hasty retreat out of the building, to the safety of the car. There, I spent the next three and a half hours listening to the car radio, sipping my orangeade, and eating crisps.

Just before eleven o'clock, Winky and Bella appeared. The two of them were making slow progress across the car park, probably because of the huge trophy they were carrying. I opened the rear door, and helped them to put it on the back seat.

"I took first prize." Winky looked suitably smug. "What do you think to the trophy?"

"Very tasteful."

"And, there's the small matter of a cheque for FIVE THOUSAND POUNDS!"

"Five grand? Do I get a share?"

"Why would I give you a share?" He laughed.

"Because I brought you here. If I hadn't, you wouldn't have been able to take part in the tournament."

"You're right. It was good of you to provide transport, and I don't want to appear ungrateful."

"Do I get a cut then?"

"No. Something much better than that. When we get back to the office, Bella will take a photo of you, me, and the trophy. I'll get a print framed especially for you."

"You're so generous."

"I know. I can't help myself."

Chapter 4

I'd been working my way through Sir Cuthbert's list of employees, most of whom I'd been able to interview at the house. I was now catching up with the last few by visiting them at their homes. The next one on my list was Roger Tyler, the head gardener.

"Who are you?" he asked through the half open door of his flat.

"My name is Jill Gooder. I'm working for Sir Cuthbert Cutts. He gave me your name."

"Why did he give you *my* name?"

The door was fully open now, and he stood towering above me. Roger Tyler had ginger hair, and a black moustache. It wasn't a good look.

"I'm interviewing all employees, past and present."

"Is it about that vase that's gone missing?"

"You heard about it, then?"

"Everyone at the house knows about it. We're not meant to say anything in case the papers get a hold of it."

"Do you have any idea what could have happened to it?"

"How would I know? It's not like I even work inside the house. I spend all my time in the gardens. I'd be the last person to know."

"I thought maybe you'd heard rumours, or talked to the other staff about it."

"I don't listen to rumours, and I certainly don't talk to the other staff. Look, I have to go out in a few minutes. I really don't have time for this."

With that, he shut the door in my face. As I turned to leave, I noticed a woman about to let herself into the flat next door.

"I wouldn't take it personally." She'd obviously seen Tyler slam the door in my face. "He's like that with everyone."

"Do you know him well?"

"No, and I wouldn't want to. He's always been the same—very standoffish, but recently he's got even worse."

"How do you mean?"

"He's so full of himself. Thinks he's a cut above everyone else. He's only a gardener, after all. He drives around in that posh car of his, and thinks he's really something."

She pointed to a green Porsche in the car park below. It looked as if it had just come out of the showroom. How could he possibly afford a car like that? Maybe Roger Tyler was worth a closer look?

***

The next name on Sir Cuthbert's list was that of Phillip Beaman who had been his butler until twelve months earlier when he'd apparently resigned unexpectedly.

Unlike Roger Tyler, Mr Beaman was very amenable, and was more than happy to invite me into his apartment.

"I'm not really sure how I can help," he said. "You realise I left Sir Cuthbert's employ almost a year ago?"

"Yes, but if you could answer a few questions, that would be most helpful."

"Of course."

"While you were working at the house, were you ever aware of any antiques going missing?"

"No, nothing."

"How did you come to hear about the vase, seeing as you no longer work there?"

"I made many good friends while I was at the house. I still see some of them from time to time."

"Are you still in contact with Roger Tyler, the gardener?"

"No. The indoor and outdoor staff rarely mixed, and besides, he and I never really did hit it off."

"I'm curious why you chose to leave after so many years. You're obviously too young to retire. Was there any particular reason?"

He shrugged. "Not really. I just felt it was time for a change."

"Where are you working now?"

"I'm *not* at the moment. I thought I'd take some time off to enjoy my hobbies, and to travel a little."

The apartment where Phillip Beaman lived was in one of the more expensive parts of Washbridge. The rent must have been extremely high.

"Do you have any plans to return to work?"

"Eventually, but I'm not in any hurry. I've always been careful with money. I have some savings, so I can afford to relax and enjoy life for a while."

"Is there anyone among Sir Cuthbert's staff who you think might know anything about the missing vase? Anyone in particular you think I should speak to?"

"No. They're all thoroughly decent people. It came as quite a shock when I heard about the incident."

"Okay. Well, thank you very much for your time. Here's my card. Perhaps you would give me a call if anything comes to mind?"

"Of course."

Although much friendlier than Roger Tyler, Phillip Beaman now also had a question mark next to his name. He'd said he was living on savings, but the rent on his apartment would have soon eaten into those. And yet, he'd seemed completely unconcerned.

***

"Jill!" I almost jumped out of my seat, and Winky actually *did* fall out of the window sill. Mrs G obviously had no idea how an intercom worked. She was shouting so loudly that I could hear her through the wall, *and* through the intercom.

"Yes, Mrs G?"

"I've got a man out here to see you. Shall I tell him to go away?"

"Who is he?"

"What's your name?" I heard her yell at the visitor. "He says his name's Drake."

"Oh, right. Send him in, please."

I hadn't been expecting his visit, and my first thought was that maybe something had happened to his brother, Raven. But, as soon as he walked in, I could tell everything was okay because he had a huge smile on his face.

"Hi." He gave me a quick peck on the cheek.

Wow! Things were looking up. I caught a glimpse of Winky out of the corner of my eye. He was pretending to make himself vomit. I ignored him.

"I've been doing some thinking," Drake said. "Now I know that Raven is okay, it's time I moved on with my own life. I thought I'd look for a property here in Washbridge. It would be nice to have a base here where I can stay from time to time."

Oh dear. Much as I enjoyed his company, I kind of liked knowing that Drake was in Candlefield. I already had Jack in Washbridge, and of course, Luscious Luther. If Drake got a place here too, that could make things a little awkward. Not that I was actually dating *any* of them. But, as always, I lived in hope.

"That would be nice." I managed a smile. "Have you found anywhere yet?"

"No. That's why I popped in to see you. I don't really know my way around Washbridge all that well. I thought maybe, when you have the time, you could come up with suggestions of areas to look at, and maybe even check out some properties with me?"

"Sure, but I'm a bit busy at the moment." I caught Winky looking at me again. If he said anything, I'd kill him. "There are a few cases which need my attention, but as soon as I've got those out of the way, I'd be glad to help."

"That's great. Well, I don't want to keep you from your work. I'll call you later then."

"Sure."

And with that he was gone.

I could sense Winky's one eye burning into me.
"Why are you giving me *that* look?" I said.
"A lot of work on?" He scoffed. "Since when?"

"I've got the missing vase case."

"Wow! A missing vase. You get all the prestigious jobs."

"Sir Cuthbert considers it priceless."

"*You're* priceless. Did you hear yourself? 'I'm too busy', 'I've got so many cases on'. Why didn't you just tell him the truth? You're already struggling to juggle two men here in Washbridge, and three would be too difficult."

"I am not *juggling* any men. I just happen to have two men friends here, and one in Candlefield."

"So, that would be three then?"

"Yeah, but—"

"You had a go at me because I'm involved with Cindy *and* Bella. Now let me see—Cindy plus Bella equals two. The last time I checked, two was less than three, so I don't think you're in any position to criticise."

"Oh be quiet. It's none of your business."

"Maybe I should let each of your men friends know about the other men in your life?"

"You wouldn't do that."

"Wouldn't I?"

"Salmon?"

"Red, not pink."

"Obviously."

***

"I'm so glad I caught you," Luther Stone said, in his *oh so sexy* voice.

"Hello, Luther." I hadn't seen him since the *misunderstanding* over the 'dinner date' at my place. I'd been keeping a low profile since then.

"I have a favour to ask you, Jill."

"Oh?" Anything for you, Luther. Your wish is my command.

"I'm having a new brochure designed for my business, and I thought it would be nice to include some photographs and quotes from existing customers. I realise that you're a relatively new customer, but you are very photogenic—"

Oh my, Luther Stone thinks I'm photogenic!

"I wondered if you'd allow me to use your photograph, and maybe also to include a quote from you in my brochure? If it's not too much trouble, that is?"

"No trouble at all. I'd be happy to do it. I'm free right now. I'd just need to go and get changed—"

"No, no. We don't need to do it right this moment. I've got a few things to organise first, but I thought if you were willing, I could let you know when, and maybe we could do it at my place?"

His place? He was inviting me to his place! "Yes, I suppose that would be okay," I said nonchalantly. Just try stopping me.

"Good. It's a date then. I'll let you know as soon as I've got things organised. Bye, Jill."

Luther Stone had just said the word 'date'. You heard him, didn't you? He definitely said 'date'. There was no misunderstanding this time. I had a date with Luther Stone! Yay!

Chapter 5

Barry came rushing up to me as soon as I reached the top of the stairs.

"Hi, Jill! I'm so pleased to see you!"

"Lovely to see you too, Barry. How's things?"

I was surprised he hadn't already asked me to take him for a walk. It was usually the first thing he said whenever he saw me.

"Jill?"

"Yes, Barry?"

"There's something I want to ask you."

Ah, here it comes — the walk.

"Can I have a friend?"

"A friend?"

"Yes. I'm all alone when you're not here."

"You have the twins."

"Yes but, I want someone who'll be with me all the time."

Now I felt bad. Aunt Lucy and the twins took him for walks when I wasn't around, but he still spent a lot of time by himself. I assumed he wanted another dog to keep him company.

"So, can I have a friend, Jill? Can I? Please! Can I, please?"

"I'm not sure there's enough room for two dogs in this flat, Barry."

"I don't want a dog."

"Oh? What do you want, then?"

"A hamster."

"Huh?"

"You know — they're a bit like mice."

"Yeah, I know what a hamster is, but why do you want one?"

"Well, they're very cute, and they're very interesting. Did you know they go on a wheel and run round and round in circles?"

"Yes, I've seen them do that."

"So, can I have one then, Jill, please? Can I have a hamster for a friend?"

I wasn't sure the twins would be keen on the idea, and I had my own reservations. I decided the best course of action was to try to take his mind off it.

"Why don't we go for a walk, Barry?"

"A walk! Yes, let's go for a walk. Can we go to the park? I love the park."

"Yes, we'll go to the park. I'll get your lead."

Phew! That seemed to have done the trick. Hopefully, he'd forget about the hamster.

***

After our walk in the park, I made my way over to Aunt Lucy's. She didn't look very happy.

"Are you okay?" I asked.

"Yes, I'm fine." She didn't sound it.

"What's wrong?"

"Did you know the twins aren't talking to me?"

"Yes, they told me. I explained that you had no idea that the cakes were for Miles."

"So did I, but they don't believe me. I'm hurt that they think I would knowingly do something like that." She forced a smile. "Anyway, forget them. I have some news."

"What's that?"

"Lester and I are going to get married next year."

"That's great!" I gave her a hug. "Do the twins know?"

"No, and I don't see why I should tell them after the way they've been acting. You won't tell them, will you, Jill?"

"Not if you don't want me to."

"They can jolly well wait to find out."

"How is Lester, anyway?"

"He's fine. He's back to his old self. In fact, I would say he's a better wizard now than he was before. But don't tell Grandma I said that."

"Don't worry—I won't."

Aunt Lucy's phone rang. Within moments of her answering it, I could sense it wasn't good news.

"What's wrong?" I asked when she'd ended the call.

"That was a friend of mine, Cynthia Pride. Her daughter's gone missing in Washbridge."

I could see Aunt Lucy was worried, so I agreed to accompany her to her friend's house.

***

Cynthia Pride looked pale and drawn; her husband was doing his best to reassure her.

"Cynthia, this is my niece, Jill," Aunt Lucy said.

Cynthia stood and came towards us.

"Please help me find Gertie," she said, through her tears. "Please."

"Can you tell me exactly what happened?"

Her husband stepped forward. "It would probably be best if I talk to you."

Cynthia sat back down on the sofa.

"Shall we go through to the kitchen?" Mr Pride said.

Aunt Lucy stayed with her friend on the sofa while I followed Mr Pride.

"How much do you already know?" he said.

"Nothing really—just that your daughter is missing."

"I blame myself. I had the chance of a job working in the human world—in Washbridge. It was too good an opportunity to turn down, so I persuaded Cynthia that we should move there. Gertie wasn't very happy about it, but I thought she'd come around. This morning, she asked if she could take two of her friends to Washbridge to show them around. How could we say no? We knew how hard all of this was for her, so we agreed. She'd been to Washbridge with us a few times, so she knew her way around."

"How did she disappear?"

"Gertie and her friends were doing a little shopping. For some reason, she stayed outside one of the shops while her friends went inside. When they came out, Gertie had disappeared. They waited for a while in case she'd gone into another shop, but after an hour, there was still no sign of her, so they came back to Candlefield to tell us."

"Have you been in touch with the police in Washbridge?"

"Yes, we contacted them straight away. We spoke to a man called Jack Maxwell."

"I know Jack."

"He seems to be on top of it. He said he would mobilise all available officers. Your Aunt Lucy had told Cynthia about you, and we thought that, as you're a witch living in Washbridge, you might be able to help."

As he spoke, I could see the strain beginning to tell on

him. He was just about holding it together.

"I'll do everything I can. I'll need to speak to the friends who were with her when she disappeared. Can that be arranged?"

He nodded. "They live close by. I'll give their parents a ring now."

While he did that, I put in a call to Jack Maxwell.

"Jack, it's Jill." I still hated how that sounded.

"Jill, I'm rather busy at the moment."

"Just hear me out, please. Are you dealing with the missing girl case? Gertie Pride?"

"Yes. How did you know about that?"

"My Aunt Lucy is a friend of the girl's mother. She's asked me to help."

"There's nothing you can do. I've got all available officers on it. I understand she comes from out of town?"

"That's right." I didn't elaborate. How could I?

"I have to go," he said. "There's a lot going on here. They even want me to talk to some kind of paranormal consultant."

"A what?"

"Yeah, that was my reaction. It's a new initiative the powers-that-be have dreamed up. Whenever there's a missing child, there are certain procedures we have to follow, and the latest crazy idea is to bring in a paranormal consultant. Apparently, they believe that she may somehow be able to locate the missing girl. It's absolute nonsense. Anyway, I've got to go."

"Jack—"

He'd already gone.

***

Alan Pride had managed to get Gertie's two friends over to the house. I asked if I could be alone with them; their parents didn't have any objections. The two girls, Juniper and Holly, didn't appear to be too shaken up.

"Are you both alright?"

"I'm okay," Juniper said.

"It must have been quite a shock."

"It was," Holly said. "I don't ever want to go back to the human world again. It's horrible."

"Can you talk me through exactly what happened?"

They looked at each other, and then Juniper began.

"We were walking down the street with Gertie. She said she knew a coffee bar where you can play drums and tambourines."

"Yes, I know the one you mean. I've been there myself."

"We thought it would be fun. We were on our way there when we saw a shop which sold vinyl records. Holly and I wanted to look inside, but Gertie wasn't bothered — she said she'd wait outside for us. We were only in there a few minutes, but when we came out, she'd gone. We thought she'd probably gone into another shop, so we waited for her, but she never came back, so we magicked ourselves back to Candlefield, and told our parents what had happened."

"How was Gertie before she disappeared?"

"Okay." Juniper shrugged.

"How did she feel about moving to Washbridge?"

"She said she was looking forward to it," Juniper said.

"Are you sure?"

"Yeah. She was, wasn't she, Holly?"

"Yeah, definitely. She was looking forward to it."

I gently quizzed the two girls for a little longer, but wasn't able to extract any more useful information from them. After they'd left, something began to bug me. Neither of them had seemed particularly upset when they spoke to me. I would have expected two girls of their age, whose friend had just disappeared, to be traumatised. And when I'd asked them how Gertie felt about the move to Washbridge, their response had seemed rehearsed. Something just wasn't right.

I had a hunch, so I made a call.

"Daze? Where are you and Blaze at the moment?"

"In Candlefield. We're between jobs."

"Is there any chance you could do me a little favour?"

"Sure."

I quickly briefed her on what I wanted the pair of them to do.

***

After I'd spoken to Daze, I spent a few more minutes with Alan Pride. I asked him to talk me through the route he, his wife and Gertie had taken when they'd visited Washbridge together.

"How will that help?" He seemed agitated. "That's not when she disappeared."

"I know. Just humour me, please."

He gave me the information I needed even though he obviously thought it was a waste of time.

Moments later, I magicked myself back to Washbridge. I now had a good idea of the route the Prides had taken, and I wanted to check out the CCTV coverage of the area. That would be easier said than done because the local council were responsible for CCTV, and I'd had dealings with those 'jobsworths' before. Still, I had my methods.

"Good morning." I tried to sound as bright and breezy as possible.

"Yes?" The middle-aged man behind the desk looked as if he'd been slapped in the face with a frying pan. "Can I help you?"

"My name is Jill Gooder, and I'm doing an audit for the government on CCTV coverage. I need to speak to your control staff."

"Do you have an appointment?"

"No, but—"

"Do you have an ID card?"

"No, but—"

"No appointment, no ID, no can do."

"But I'm on a special fact-finding—"

"Goodbye."

I left the building, made myself invisible, and followed the next person back inside. While the visitor was busy talking to 'Happy' behind the desk, I slipped past them, along the corridor, and up a flight of stairs. I'd been to the control room before on a previous case, but on that occasion I hadn't known I was a witch, so I'd had to go through the proper channels. Doing it this way was much easier. Yay for being a witch!

When I reached the control room door, I looked through the glass panel, and saw the two controllers: a middle-aged man, and a woman about ten years his junior. They were kissing passionately when they should have been monitoring the screens.

I could have some fun here. Snigger!

I knocked on the door; they both jumped back in their seats. Although I was standing with my face pressed to the glass panel, they couldn't see me. The woman looked flustered; the man even more so. I knocked again. They exchanged a glance, and then the man walked slowly over and opened the door.

"There's no one here," he said.

While he had the door open, I sneaked past him into the control room.

"Someone must have knocked." The woman still looked worried.

"Well there's nobody here now. Look—"

"I told you, Jason. We can't keep doing this. Someone will catch us."

"You worry too much."

"You won't say that when we get sacked."

"We won't get sacked. Nobody ever got sacked from here. You know that."

The man returned to his seat, and tried to put his arm around her, but she pushed him away. She was obviously still nervous, and kept glancing towards the door.

I had to get them both out of the office long enough for me to check the tapes. But how? Then, I had a brainwave. I created an illusion which caused them to think that the waste paper basket in the corner of the room was actually a huge dog, which started barking at them.

"How did that get in here?" the woman said, edging back in her seat.

"I don't know but it doesn't look very friendly."

The dog moved a little closer to them. Its teeth were

bared, and it was snarling. They slid out of their seats, and crept towards the door. Once through the door, they made a run for it. That was my chance. I took a seat, grabbed the mouse, and brought up the on-screen menu. It was easy to find the coverage for the day in question, and I knew exactly which cameras I wanted to check. It took me only a few minutes to spot Gertie Pride and her parents walking along the street. I watched her every step of the way as she moved from one camera to the next. Sure enough, every time she went past a camera, she appeared to stare straight at it, and then she tapped something into her phone. Her parents were so busy looking around and talking to one another that they didn't notice the only thing their daughter seemed interested in was the CCTV cameras.

Just as I'd suspected.

Chapter 6

I met up with Daze and Blaze in Cuppy C.

"What's wrong with this colour?" Blaze frowned.

"It *is* rather orange," I said.

"Rather?" Daze couldn't take her eyes off it. "It's not *rather* anything. You'll glow in the dark."

I thought Blaze might be offended by Daze's comments. Quite the opposite—he seemed quite pleased.

"I would, wouldn't I? The luminous look suits me, don't you think, Jill?"

"I—err—suppose."

"It has to go." Daze thumped the table. "No assistant of mine is going to wear that thing."

"But—I—"

"But nothing. Get it changed by tomorrow, or I'll have to take drastic action."

Blaze's eyes widened and he glanced at me. Daze hadn't specified what the *drastic action* would be, and I knew Blaze wouldn't want to find out.

"Anyway, Jill," Daze said. "We followed the two girls as you asked. They must have suspected they'd be followed because they split up and took quite different routes all around Candlefield. I was beginning to think the girl I was following wasn't going anywhere in particular, but she eventually ended up at Black Woods. It's an area to the east of Candlefield which is popular with families with children. I'd no sooner arrived there than I saw Blaze and the other girl. The two girls met up and disappeared into one of the caves. We didn't follow them inside—we just watched and waited from a safe distance. They were in there for no more than fifteen minutes, and then they left. We can show you the cave if you like."

"Thanks, but there's no need. If you'll give me directions, I'll go over there and take a look."

I was a little peckish, so after Daze and Blaze had left, I grabbed a blueberry muffin on my way out.

"Can I pay for this later?" I asked Pearl. "I don't have any cash on me."

"No problem. We'll put it on your account. You do realise how many blueberry muffins are *already* on your account, do you, Jill?"

"Err—three or four maybe?"

"Three or four dozen, more like."

"No! I can't have eaten that many."

"I'm afraid so."

Oh bum.

***

It was the first time I'd visited Black Woods. Its name made it sound quite scary, but in fact it was quite a pleasant spot. It was quite chilly, so there weren't many people around.

I made my way on foot along a trail through the woods which eventually led to a clearing at the bottom of a hillside. Daze had given me directions to the cave in question. Just as she'd warned, it was pitch black inside. Maybe I should have brought Blaze, and his luminous catsuit. In his absence, I used my phone to light the way. After a few metres, I realised I no longer needed it because there seemed to be some kind of light source coming from deeper in the cave.

My every footstep seemed to echo. I was beginning to wonder if this was such a good idea—maybe I should have asked Daze and Blaze to come with me. Could this be some kind of elaborate trap? I was approaching a bend in the cave when someone jumped out.

"Who are you?" she said. "What are you doing here?"

"Looking for you. I assume you're Gertie Pride?"

"How did you know?"

"Because your mother and father are worried sick. I'm Jill Gooder. I'm a private investigator, and they asked me to find you."

"How did you know I was here? I thought they'd be looking for me in Washbridge."

"I thought that was your plan, but you gave yourself away."

"What do you mean?"

"When you were with your parents in Washbridge, you spent most of the time staring at CCTV cameras, and making notes on your phone. I assume you were trying to find the blind spots so you'd know where to stage the disappearance. Do you realise how worried your mother and father are?"

"They can't be *that* worried about me or they wouldn't make me live with humans, would they? All my friends are here in Candlefield. I'm a witch, not a human! I don't want to live in Washbridge."

"Look, Gertie—I understand what you're going through."

"No you don't! How can you?"

"I was raised in the human world. In fact, I thought I *was* a human until quite recently. It was only when my birth mother died that I discovered I was a witch."

"That must have been pretty weird." She looked genuinely surprised.

"It was *very* weird—and a little scary. I've lived in the human world all of my life, and I can tell you that humans aren't all that different from sups. Sure, there are some nasty humans, but there are some nasty sups too. I enjoy living in both worlds. You should give it a chance; you might surprise yourself and discover you actually like it. Just make sure your parents know that you want to keep in touch with your friends in Candlefield."

"They probably won't let me after what I've done."

"I'm sure they will. Look, if you like, I'll talk to your parents, and explain what happened."

"I'm still going to miss my friends though."

"They'll be able to visit, and maybe even stay over with you in Washbridge. It'll be an adventure for them too. I have two cousins here in Candlefield. They own Cuppy C, the cake shop and tea room. Do you know it?"

"I've seen it."

"They're witches, and they love spending time in Washbridge. I'm sure your friends will too. And you'll make lots of friends at your new school."

"How can you know that? What if no one likes me?"

"Why wouldn't they? And besides, being a witch does have certain magical advantages."

"We're not allowed to use magic in the human world, are we?"

"You're not allowed to let humans *know* you're a witch, but there are still lots of ways to use magic without them finding out."

"Really?"

"Definitely. I often use magic in Washbridge."

"Don't you get in trouble?"

"I haven't yet. But you have to be careful. You can't go around turning your classmates into frogs."

"That would be funny!"

"It might be, but it would also be pretty obvious that you were using magic. You've got to be a little subtler."

"I guess so."

"So what do you say? Shall I talk to your mum and dad, and let them know you're okay?"

She nodded.

"Why don't you come back with me to Cuppy C. My cousins sell the best blueberry muffins in Candlefield."

"Do they have chocolate ones?"

"Yes, of course. We'll get you a muffin and something to drink, and you can meet my dog, Barry, if you like."

"I love dogs. What kind is he?"

"A daft one. He's a labradoodle. He's adorable, but not the smartest. I'll leave you at Cuppy C with my cousins and Barry while I go and talk to your parents. Once I've smoothed things over with them, I'll bring them to you. How does that sound?"

"Okay, I guess. Thanks."

I took Gertie to Cuppy C, bought her a double chocolate muffin and a milkshake, and then took her upstairs. Barry was all over her like a rash.

As soon as she was settled in, I made a call to Cynthia and Alan Pride, and arranged to meet them at Aunt Lucy's. My next call was to Jack Maxwell to let him know Gertie was safe and well, and that he could stand down his men. Before he had the chance to ask any awkward questions, I told him I had a 'feline-emergency' and ended the call.

"Is she okay?" Cynthia came rushing through the door.

"Yes, she's fine. She's with my cousins."

"Where was she?" Alan said.

"Right here, in Candlefield. Look, why don't I tell you what happened, and then we'll go and see her."

"But you're sure she's okay?"

"She's absolutely fine, honestly. As we speak, she's eating a chocolate muffin and playing with my dog."

"Oh thank goodness." Cynthia began to cry.

Alan put his arm around his wife's shoulder. "It's okay, dear. She's all right. Everything's going to be okay now."

I gave them the bullet-point version, highlighting Gertie's concerns about going to live in the human world, and her fears that she would lose touch with her friends. I also explained how she'd staged the disappearance by checking for CCTV blind spots in Washbridge, and that her friends had been in on it all along.

"She figured if she could convince you that the human world was a dangerous place to live, you would change your plans."

"Maybe we should," said Cynthia.

"We can't. If we don't move now, I won't have a job, and we'll be broke."

"But if she really doesn't want to go?"

"Look," I interrupted. "I've spoken to Gertie, and told her about my own experience of living in both worlds. I think she's coming round to the idea, but I said I'd speak to you on her behalf. She wants to be absolutely sure that she'll be able to keep in touch with her friends here in Candlefield."

"Of course she will! We always said she could."

"You need to make it clear that she'll be allowed to move between the two worlds as often as she likes, within reason."

"Is that a good idea?" Cynthia said. "We thought it best that she should concentrate on getting used to living in the human world."

"If Gertie knows she can visit Candlefield whenever she wants to, it'll put her mind at ease. Then she can relax and slowly integrate with the humans."

"What do you think, Alan?" Cynthia said, wiping a tear from her eye.

"I think Jill's right. Maybe we've focussed too much on trying to get her to fit in with the humans. She's a witch, and she'll always be a witch. We have to reassure her that she won't lose her old life or friends."

With that settled, I took the Prides to Cuppy C where there was a tearful reunion.

My job there was done.

Chapter 7

Back in Washbridge, there was an awful lot of noise coming from the outer office. I didn't know what Mrs G was up to, but I sensed it wasn't anything good.

"What's that racket out there?" Winky said. "What's the bag lady's twisted sister up to now?"

"I don't know, but I'm going to find out."

Mrs V's desk was piled high with scarves and socks. On the floor, next to the desk, was a pile of black rubbish sacks.

"Mrs G, what are you doing?"

"I'm getting rid of all this rubbish. Did you know the desk and filing cabinet are full of scarves and socks? I'm going to throw them out to make some room in here."

"You can't do that."

"Why ever not?"

"Your sister made those."

"She shouldn't be knitting during office hours. Doesn't she know you have a business to run? I'm surprised you let her get away with it. No wonder your business is going downhill."

"My business is doing okay."

"That's not what the books say."

"You've been looking at my books?"

"Someone has to, dear. You obviously don't. Do you know you're almost up to the limit on your overdraft? While I'm here, the least I can do is to knock this business into shape for you. I'll just get rid of this lot, and then you and I can have a meeting to discuss your strategy *going forward*. How does that sound?"

Like my idea of hell. "That sounds great, but—err—I've

just remembered I've got an—err—appointment. A meeting. A meeting-appointment. Right now. In fact—five minutes ago. Got to go. Bye."

I had to get rid of Mrs G. I couldn't put up with her for another minute. What would Mrs V say when she came back and found out that all of her scarves and socks had been thrown out? She'd kill her sister.

I walked the streets of Washbridge for a while. I couldn't go back to the office; the last thing I needed was a strategy meeting with Mrs G. Eventually, I decided to pop into Ever A Wool Moment, to have a chat with Kathy. Hopefully Grandma wouldn't be around.

I found Kathy in the tea room which was as busy as ever.

"Where's Grandma?" I said.

"In the back. I don't know what she's up to, but she's been in there for hours. Something's going on. I just hope she hasn't come up with another sales initiative. I've got enough on my plate what with the Everlasting Wool, the One-Size Needles and 'Ever' membership. I can't cope with anything else."

"I did warn you."

"I know. Don't rub it in. Anyway, what are you doing here? I didn't think you'd want to be anywhere near your grandmother."

"I had to get out of the office. Mrs V's gone missing. Her sister's taken over her job temporarily, and she's driving me crazy. She's been trying to tell me how to run my business, and now she wants us to have a *strategy* meeting. Worst of all, she's going to throw out all of Mrs V's scarves and socks."

"Oh no she isn't," someone yelled.

The sudden interruption took us both by surprise. I looked around to see the same old biddy who'd been there the last time I was in the tea room. She stood up, and removed her hat, wig, and glasses.

"Mrs V?"

"What's that sister of mine up to?"

"Never mind that." I stared at her in disbelief. "What are *you* up to? I've been worried about you. I thought something might have happened to you."

"I've been hiding from G. I said in my note that you shouldn't worry. I didn't want to be around while she was here."

"How long have you been hanging out in here?"

"Every day since I found out G was coming. I thought I'd better wear a disguise, so your sister didn't recognise me. What's G doing?"

"When I left, she'd taken all of your scarves and socks out of the desk and the filing cabinet, and she was about to put them in bin bags."

"Over my dead body," said Mrs V. "We have to stop her, Jill."

"We? What am I supposed to do?"

"You have to get rid of her."

"She won't listen to me. If I go back there, she'll insist on having a strategy meeting."

I turned to Kathy. "You do something."

"Me—what can I do?"

"I've got an idea." Mrs V grinned.

"This is never going to work," Kathy said.

"Of course it will," I insisted. "You're good at this sort

of thing."

"Flattery will get you nowhere, Jill. I don't see why *you* can't make the phone call."

"She'll recognise my voice."

"What am I supposed to say?"

"We've told you what to say. Go on—just pick up the phone and ring her."

Kathy sighed, but she made the phone call anyway.

"Hello, is that Mrs G?" Kathy had put on her 'Sunday best' voice. "Oh good. This is Pauletta Peters from Wool TV—yes I'm very well thank you. And you? Good. I realise this is very short notice, but we have a spot on our prime time show, 'Wool World', this evening, and we'd really love to interview you, if you're available. You are? That's excellent. No, we don't want you to come to the studio. The whole point of the programme is that we interview you in your home, and get you to talk us through all of your achievements in the world of yarn. You're away from home at the moment? How disappointing. You *can* get back there? Good. You'll have to hurry because the camera crew will be making their way there shortly. Okay, well we'll see you at your place later. Thank you. Goodbye."

"That was brilliant, Kathy," Mrs V said. "Thank you so much."

"You're a natural." I patted her on the shoulder. "You should join Washbridge Am dram."

"You two owe me big time."

"What's going on out here?" Grandma came charging out of the back office. "I thought *you* were meant to be running my shop!" she shouted at Kathy. "Not chatting to your sister."

"I was just—"

"Never mind that. Get on with the subscriptions or something."

Kathy scurried away.

"And you two," Grandma said. "What do you think you're doing distracting my staff when they're supposed to be working? I have my bottom line to think of."

Mrs V shrugged and turned to me. "Thanks for that Jill. By the time I get back, the coast should be clear. Hopefully G won't have had time to throw away my scarves and socks."

"I'll walk back to the office with you." I offered.

"Just a minute, young lady," Grandma interrupted. "Annabel, you can go." She dismissed Mrs V with a wave of her hand, and then turned to me. "I want a word with you."

Great!

"Let's go in the back."

"Must we?"

"Yes, it's better that we talk in there. This is a matter of the utmost importance."

Oh no.

"Have a seat," she ordered.

"I really am quite busy."

"Have a seat."

I did as I was instructed.

"You'll no doubt be aware that Candlefield is going to the dogs," she said.

"I can't say I'd noticed."

"You'll just have to take my word for it. I've lived there long enough to know, and I'm telling you, the place is falling to pieces. And, do you know *why*?"

I had a feeling she was going to tell me.

"I'll tell you why."

See—I knew it.

"The town council doesn't have a clue. It's about time they had someone on there who actually knows their ass from their elbow."

"And that someone would be?"

"That *someone* would be *me*, of course. A vacancy has arisen because Ben Benjamin has decided to retire, so there's going to be an election. I intend to stand."

"Well that's great. I'm really pleased. I'm sure you'll do a terrific job. But anyway, as I said, I am quite—"

"Sit down. I haven't finished with you yet. I need a campaign manager, and I've decided that you're the person for the job."

"I don't know anything about election campaigns."

"You don't know anything about being a P.I., but you seem to muddle through. You just need to talk a lot, and you can certainly do that."

"I don't talk all that much."

"Be quiet. So, as of now, you are officially the campaign manager for Mirabel Millbright. Any questions?"

***

My head was still spinning with the election campaign when I got back to my flat that evening. As soon as I walked through the door, I heard a noise, and was immediately on my guard. Was this another attempt by TDO to get to me? I crept slowly towards the kitchen and pushed open the door.

"Mum?"

"Jill? I didn't realise you'd be back just yet."

What was she doing here? This was the second time I'd caught her in the flat—something strange was going on.

"Is everything okay, Mum?"

"Err—yes. Everything's fine."

She didn't look fine. She looked very nervous.

"I just came round to—err—ask how you felt about Lucy getting married."

"I'm very pleased for her. Lester is really nice. I'm sure they'll be very happy together."

"Good. I just thought I'd check. I'll get off then, bye." And with that, she disappeared.

Huh? What was that all about? Why wouldn't I be okay with Aunt Lucy getting married? It's not like Lester was some kind of evil demon. My family got crazier every day.

What I really needed was a nice cup of tea and some custard creams. I switched the kettle on, and while it was boiling, I took out the custard cream box.

It was empty!

There had definitely been some in there—I remembered putting them in. This was the second time this had happened recently.

Hold on a minute!

The last time I'd found the custard cream box empty was just after I'd found my mother in the flat. What a coincidence! I was beginning to smell a rat.

"Mum," I shouted. "Mum!"

She reappeared, looking very sheepish. "You called, Jill?"

"What do you call this?" I said, pointing to the empty box.

"I think it's called Tupperware, isn't it?"

"That's not what I mean, and you know it."

"I'm sorry," she said. "I hadn't intended to eat them all. I had one, then two, and then I lost count."

"Why do you keep raiding my stock of custard creams? Is there a shortage in the ghost world?"

"Alberto's been on my case. He said I've been eating too many, so I promised that I'd cut back. And I have — sort of."

"So, you've cut back on eating *your* custard creams, but now you're eating *mine* instead?"

"When you put it like that — it sounds kind of bad. I'm sorry — I'll buy you some more."

"I don't mind you eating them, but I'd rather you didn't eat every last one. What would Alberto think if he knew?"

"You're right. I feel like I've been cheating on him."

"I'm not sure cheating with a custard cream counts."

"Still, I promise I won't steal any more. Or if I do, I'll only take one at a time."

Chapter 8

When I set off for the office the next morning, I walked straight into Betty. I'd been avoiding her for a while because I thought she'd be grieving over the loss of her one true love, Norman, the mastermind.

"Morning, Jill." She seemed very bright and breezy. Either she was over Norman, or she'd forgiven him for favouring the bottle top conference over her birthday.

"Morning. You seem very chipper this morning. Are you and Norman back together?"

"Norman? Huh. Don't mention *him* to me; stupid man and his bottle tops. I can't think what I ever saw in him in the first place."

Me neither. "Well, you certainly seem to be over him."

"I am. Between you and me, Jill, I have my eye on another man."

"Really? Already?"

"I can't say too much at the moment," she said, in little more than a whisper. "But I think he may be sweet on me too."

"Really?" Perhaps I should take up collecting sea shells. Apparently, it was a sure fire way to attract men.

"Yes, he's really hot."

"Hotter than Norman?"

"Anybody's hotter than Norman."

That much was true.

"This guy is a *real* man, if you know what I mean." She gave me a knowing wink. Either that, or she had something in her eye.

"That's great."

"You know him, actually."

"I do?"

She looked around to check that the coast was clear. "It's our new neighbour, Luther Stone. I think he fancies me."

I was gobsmacked. Luther Stone fancy Betty? How delusional could one person be? What do you mean, I should know? If Luther Stone fancied anyone in this building, it was me — not Betty Longbottom.

"Are you absolutely sure about that?"

"Oh yes. You should see the way he looks at me. It's like he's undressing me with those sexy eyes of his."

I was lost for words. What? It happens occasionally.

This couldn't be happening. Luther was all mine, and I didn't intend to share him with Betty Longbottom.

"I really think you should stay away from Luther, Betty."

"Why?" She looked shocked. "What's wrong with him?"

"He's — err — I've heard things about him."

"What kind of things?"

"Bad things."

"What do you mean?"

"Err — I shouldn't really say. I don't want to repeat gossip."

"You can't just leave it at that."

"I — err — heard that he's — wanted by the police."

"Why? What's he done?"

"Err — money laundering for a major crime syndicate — so I heard. I should stay well clear. There might even be a contract out on him." I was digging myself into a deeper and deeper hole.

"Morning ladies!" Luther said.

Oh no!

Betty looked at him with new eyes. "Morning," she said, coldly.

"Morning, Luther," I said. "Sorry, I've got to run. Bye."

I shot out of the building, jumped in the car and sped off. I prayed that Betty wouldn't confront Luther about his money laundering operation.

***

Terry Brown was Sir Cuthbert's chef. I'd arranged to meet him at his home; a two-bedroom semi on the west side of Washbridge.

"Jill?" He greeted me at the door. "Come in. Take a seat."

It was like walking into an antique shop. All of the furniture, pictures and ornaments looked valuable, and seemed somewhat out of place in such a modest house.

"Are you a collector, Terry?" I said.

"How did you guess?" He grinned. "My parents used to have an antiques shop. I was brought up around antiques, and I guess I acquired a taste for them. It's not easy, though, on my salary."

"You seem to be doing okay."

"Thanks, but this collection has taken me many years to put together."

"You heard about the vase, I assume?"

"I did. It's terrible. I've always been worried that someone might break in here, and steal my pieces. I have an alarm fitted, but that's not likely to stop a determined burglar."

"Do you have insurance?"

"Yes. It costs a small fortune, and what good is it anyway? I'd get a pay-out, but I'd never be able to replace these." He looked around the room.

I found Terry to be very open. Over tea and cakes, he answered all of my questions without any hesitation. I considered myself a pretty good judge of character, and he struck me as a genuine guy. Still, I couldn't help but wonder how he'd managed to accumulate such a collection of antiques on what must have been a modest salary.

On my way out, one piece in particular caught my eye. It looked familiar, but I couldn't think why. It was a gold plate on which was engraved the head of a serpent. Where had I seen it before?

***

I was doing a shift behind the counter at Cuppy C, and beginning to think that I'd got the hang of this tea room lark.

"Hey, Amber," I said. "Don't you think I'm getting better at this?"

She gave me a look, then turned to Pearl, and they both giggled.

"Seriously though? I'm doing okay, aren't I?"

"Yeah, you're doing really—" Pearl hesitated. "*Okay*."

"Yeah, extremely—err—*average*," Amber said.

"Exceptionally average." Pearl nodded.

"You two are horrible."

"We're only kidding. You're definitely improving, but to be honest you make a much better witch than you do a tea room assistant. We still love you though!"

"Yeah, just don't give up your day job."

Obviously, I wasn't doing as well as I'd thought. "I haven't seen Aunt Lucy for a while. Is she still full of the we—" I caught myself.

The twins gave me a puzzled look. "What did you just say, Jill?"

"Nothing. I—err—said I haven't seen Aunt Lucy for a while."

"No, after that. You said 'is she still full of the we'—?"

"Full of the we—err—werewolf news."

"Werewolf news?" Pearl looked even more confused.

"Yes. Aunt Lucy and I often discuss werewolves—and the news appertaining to them."

"Jill? What were you really going to say?"

"Okay, okay. I wondered if she was still full of the wedding."

"Who's getting married?" the twins said, in unison.

"Aunt Lucy and Lester. I thought she might have told you. But, I'm guessing, she hasn't?"

"No, she most *definitely* has not!" Amber said.

"How come *you* know and *we* don't?" Pearl said, the outrage showing on her face.

"Probably because *I'm* talking to her. If you remember, you two stopped talking to her because of the Miles Best cakes situation."

"Entirely justified," Amber said. "So, when *is* this wedding?"

"Some time next year."

"Naturally, we'll be her bridesmaids," Pearl said.

I shrugged. "Maybe, she'll ask someone else seeing as you two aren't talking to her."

"We *are* talking to her. It was only a temporary

measure," Pearl said. "It's all forgotten now."

"So you've actually spoken to her recently, have you?"

"We've been thinking about doing, haven't we, Amber?"

"Yes. In fact, now you mention it, I think we'll go over there later today."

"And this change of heart has nothing to do with you two wanting to be bridesmaids then?"

"Of course not. Nothing at all. We'd planned to do it anyway, hadn't we, Pearl?"

"Yes, definitely."

A likely story.

While we were on a break, Amber mentioned that she hadn't seen Grandma for a while.

"Not that I'm complaining." She laughed.

"I have a horrible feeling I'm going to be seeing an awful lot of her. Did you know she's running for election to Candlefield Town Council?"

"Grandma as a local councillor? Who'd vote for her?" Pearl looked nervously around, just in case Grandma was within earshot.

"Hopefully a lot of people because I'm her campaign manager."

"Why did you volunteer to do that?" Amber looked genuinely shocked. "Are you insane?"

"Who said I volunteered? Grandma 'volunteered' me. She informed me that I was doing it, and that was that."

"Do you have any experience of that sort of thing?" Pearl said.

"None at all."

"Oh dear." They giggled. "You really *are* in trouble. If

Grandma doesn't win, guess who'll get the blame?"

"Thanks, that makes me feel much better."

***

I was driving through Washbridge when I noticed a huge poster. It was promoting the movie which Mr Ivers had mentioned: 'Full Force'.

What the—?

I hadn't realised that Rick Ryland was in it! He'd been my favourite movie star for as long as I could remember. He was *hot* with a capital 'H'. At the bottom of the poster, it said that he, along with some of the other members of the cast, would be appearing at the premiere in London. The same premiere that Mr Ivers had invited me to! The premiere that I'd said I didn't want to go to! Oh no! I couldn't let this golden opportunity pass me by.

I hammered on Mr Ivers' door. He *had* to be in or I'd cry. Come on! I hammered again. Finally, the door opened.

"Jill?" Mr Ivers looked confused, but then it probably wasn't every day he had a woman hammering on his door. "Are you okay?"

I tried to catch my breath. "Yeah—I'm fine."

"You don't look okay. You look like you've been running."

"I'm okay. I was just wondering—you mentioned the premiere of 'Full Force'."

"It doesn't look as though I'll be going. I don't have anyone to go with."

"I'll be happy to go with you."

"But, you said you were too busy."

"No, you must have misunderstood. I said that I *thought* I might be busy. It turns out that I'm free after all. Do you still have the tickets?"

"Yes, of course."

"That's great! We'll make arrangements later then."

Off I ran, back to my flat. Once inside, I let out a whoop and gave a fist pump. I was going to see Rick Ryland! Forget Luther. Forget Jack. Forget Drake. Even forget Jethro. Rick Ryland, my dream man, here I come.

Chapter 9

"There's a man in your office," Mrs V said.

"What man?"

"Something to do with extermination."

My blood ran cold. I knew Gordon Armitage was evil, but surely he hadn't sent a hit man to take out Winky? I rushed through to my office, and found a man crawling on his hands and knees, next to my desk.

"Excuse me. What do you think you're doing?"

He looked up. "I'm here about the bugs."

"Sorry?"

"The bugs. That's why I'm here."

"Reversing the order of the same words doesn't help. Why *exactly* are you here? What bugs?"

"The ones in your office. I've come to exterminate them."

"I don't have any *bugs* in my office."

He grinned. "That's what they all say. What do you call this then?" He held out his hand. On his palm was a horrible eight-legged creature.

"What *is* that?"

"Like I said—it's a bug, and I'm here to exterminate them."

"But I didn't call you."

"I was called in by the other occupants of this building. Armitage, Armitage—and something. They were concerned that they were being infested with bugs which originated from this office."

"Well, you can just tell Mr Armitage that I don't need your services, thank you very much. I'd like you to leave now!"

"Okay, on your head be it. If you don't mind living side by side with bugs that's fine by me." He stood up, and made his way out.

No sooner had he left than Winky slipped out from under the sofa.

"Has he gone?"

"Yes, I sent him packing."

"He was up to no good."

"What do you mean?"

"He might have been here on 'bug' business, but it wasn't the creepy crawly kind."

"Huh?"

"He didn't notice me, but I was watching him. He planted a 'bug' under your desk."

"A cockroach?"

"Not that kind of bug!" Winky sighed with obvious exasperation. "How did you ever become a private investigator? An electronic 'bug'—a listening device!"

"Are you sure?"

"Of course I'm sure. Any minute now it'll be activated, so we should probably stop talking." He put his paw to his lips.

I bent down and looked under the desk. Sure enough, there was a small device stuck to the underside. I nodded to Winky, and mouthed the word: Thanks.

"Mrs V," I whispered.

She was busy knitting a pair of orange socks.

"What's the matter, dear? Why are you whispering?"

"The man who just left—"

"The exterminator?"

"He planted a bug in my office."

She looked even more confused.

"A listening device."

"Why would he do that?"

"Someone wants to listen in on my conversations, and I have a feeling I know who."

"What are you going to do?"

"Here." I handed her a sheet of paper.

"What's this?"

"It's your script. You and I are going to do a little amateur dramatics."

"Really? How exciting. I was once in Romeo and Juliet, you know."

"Were you Juliet?"

"No, I was a tree."

"Right."

"I didn't have many lines."

"Still."

Once Mrs V had familiarised herself with the script, we went back into my office.

"Ready?" I mouthed.

She gave me a thumbs up.

"Mrs V, is everything organised for the cat show this afternoon?" I said, in my normal voice.

"Yes, Jill. Just as you requested. Everything's in place." She was in full-on thesp mode.

"How many people will be taking part?"

"Twenty altogether."

"Good. And did you call everyone to make sure they knew the details, and to confirm they are still coming?"

"I did. I reminded them that they should arrive at two o'clock. Are you sure there will be enough room in here for twenty cats?"

"I think so. If we move my desk back."

"I didn't think the landlord allowed animals."

"Don't worry about that. He'll never find out."

I knelt down and prised the 'bug' from under the desk. After disposing of it in the waste skip at the rear of the building, I re-joined Mrs V in the outer office.

"We're not really having twenty cats in here, are we?" Mrs V looked horrified.

"Of course not. But I have a sneaking suspicion that someone, not a million miles from here, will believe we are."

***

After a quick trip to the local charity shop, I began to put the next phase of my cunning master plan into action.

"What are you up to now?" Winky said.

"What does it look like?"

"It looks like you've lost your mind."

"Why don't you go and wave your flags around, or talk to someone on FelineSocial?"

Just after two o' clock, I heard a commotion in the outer office. Moments later, the door flew open.

"Stop! You can't go in there," Mrs V shouted.

Gordon Armitage burst through the door, followed closely by my landlord, Zac Whiteside.

"I told you, Zac," Armitage said. "She's having a cat show." He stopped dead in his tracks. "What the—?"

"Can I help you, Mr Armitage?" I treated the pair of them to my charmingest smile. What? Of course it's a word.

"Err—I thought—" Armitage spluttered.

Zac stepped forward. "Jill, I'm sorry for this interruption. Mr Armitage insisted that you were holding a *cat* show in here, but it appears he may have got that wrong." He looked around the office. Fortunately, Winky had taken the hint, and hidden under the sofa.

"It's actually a *hat* show," I said. "In aid of the local Washbridge Children's Charity. I hope you don't mind, Zac?"

I pointed to the hats which I'd purchased earlier from the charity shop. They were now displayed around the office in a rather pleasing manner. Although I do say so myself, I have a natural flair when it comes to visual merchandising.

"Not at all. A very worthy cause. A few hats never hurt anyone, did they, Mr Armitage?"

"Err—" Armitage looked at me, and I winked at him. His face flushed red with fury. He knew I'd found the listening device, but what could he say? He could hardly tell Zac that he'd been bugging my office.

"Would you like to buy a hat while you're here, Mr Armitage?"

He didn't answer. He just turned around and stormed out of the office.

"Sorry again," Zac said. "I won't trouble you any longer. Mr Armitage seems to have got a bee in his *bonnet*." He laughed. "Bonnet? Get it?"

After he'd left, Winky came sliding out from under the sofa. "You really can be quite sly, can't you?"

"I try."

***

I was at Kathy's house.

"What makes you think I'm trying to get out of it?" I put on my best innocent expression.

"I don't *think* you're trying to get out of it. I *know* you are," Kathy said. "Go on then — if you really do have a client coming to see you, what's his name?"

"Err — Mr — err —"

"See! You're lying. Look, you promised to go to the kids' party, and that's where you're going."

"Will there be clowns?"

"No. I've already told you; there aren't any clowns this year. It's Punch and Judy. Anyway, I didn't think you were scared of clowns?"

"I'm not *scared* of them." Terrified more like. "I just don't find them very funny."

"Come on, Mummy, it's time to go," Lizzie shouted.

"Can I take my drum?" Mikey was banging it as loudly as he could.

"No, you can't. I'm sick of it. You can leave it here."

"But, Mummy, I could play it and everyone could dance."

"The drum stays here — or you don't go."

Mikey reluctantly put the drum on the table.

"I still blame you for that stupid thing," Kathy said.

"How many times do I have to tell you? I didn't buy it. It was nothing to do with me."

"Hmm."

"Anyway, how come Peter gets away with not going to the party?"

"Because Pete has a *real* job. You know? One of those where you actually have to do some work."

"I have a real job. I solve important cases."

"About two a year."
"Rubbish."
"How many have you solved this year, so far?"
"Too many to recall."
"How many?"
"A lot."
"How many?"
"Definitely more than two."

***

It took a while to find a parking space at the Community Hall. The place was packed with mums, dads, grandmas, granddads and a million-and-one kids. It was going to be a long afternoon.

Once inside, I could barely hear myself think.

"How long does this go on for?" I shouted.

"We've only just walked through the door." Kathy gave me a disapproving frown.

"I was only asking."

"Probably two hours. Certainly no more than three."

"Three hours? I'll be deaf by then!"

"Stop complaining and go and get us both a drink."

"There are drinks?" That was good news at least. Maybe a little alcohol would numb my senses just enough to get me through this ordeal.

"Not the kind you're thinking of — only soft drinks. Go and get us one."

En route to the refreshments stall, I walked by the stage where the Punch and Judy booth had already been set up. As I did, I heard a familiar voice.

"Daze?"

She popped her head around the side of the booth. "Jill? What are you doing here?"

"More to the point — what are *you* doing here?"

Blaze appeared around the other side. "Hi, Jill."

"Hi, Blaze. What on earth are you two up to?"

"We're the entertainment."

"*You're* doing the Punch and Judy show?"

"Yeah," Blaze said. "I'm Judy. I wanted to be Mr Punch, but Daze wouldn't let me."

"How many jobs do you two have?"

"Only ever one at a time," Daze said. "But I get bored so easily. And besides, those dogs were driving me crazy. This is a much better gig. Puppets — nothing to it."

"Don't you have to learn a script?"

"Nah, the show is only for kids. We just improvise. As long as we get the crocodile out, throw a few sausages around, and I hit Blaze — I mean Judy — over the head with a stick a few times, the kids are happy."

"I'm not sure you can do that anymore. It's not very 'PC'.

"I'll hit him with the sausages then; no one can complain about that, surely. Anyway, what are *you* doing here?"

"My sister, Kathy, dragged me here with her kids. I didn't want to come. I hate these things; they're so noisy. I'm thinking of sneaking around the back to escape."

"That would hardly be fair to your sister, would it?"

Why was everyone guilt-tripping me? "I suppose you're right. Are the two of you working on anything interesting?"

"We're on the trail of Mona, a rogue witch if ever there was one. We've had a few run-ins with her over the years." Daze checked her watch. "Sorry, Jill. It's show time. Catch you later."

As soon as the Punch and Judy show was underway, Lizzie, Mikey and all the other kids began to shout at the puppets.

"This is a very strange Punch and Judy show," Kathy said.

"How do you mean, strange?"

"This is not the usual script."

"How would you know?"

"Because I'm a mum, and I've seen a hundred Punch and Judy shows. Trust me, this is not the usual script. Punch doesn't tell Judy to 'go sling her hook'. And he doesn't hit her with sausages."

"Perhaps it's a re-imagining?"

Chapter 10

Today was *the* day. Oh yeah! The day I got to meet my heartthrob, Rick Ryland. The man oozed sex appeal, and yours truly had a ticket for the movie premiere. There was, of course, one downside: I had to go with Mr Ivers. The train journey alone would be three whole hours. Would he notice if I pretended to go to the loo, and slipped away to find a vacant seat in another carriage?

"Hi, Jill." He beamed.

"You're looking very dapper, Mr Ivers. I haven't seen you in that suit before. Have you had it hidden away?"

"How did you guess?"

"Just a hunch." And the smell of mothballs. "I see you're sporting a cravat too."

"I've always thought cravats were rather debonair."

Not the word I would have used. But still.

"You're looking very beautiful, Jill."

I'd always said Mr Ivers had a discerning eye.

"I thought we might be travelling first class," I said, as we squeezed into the narrow seats in standard class.

"I'm afraid not. The premiere tickets were free, but I had to pay for the train tickets. Which reminds me — you owe me thirty-five pounds."

Huh?

"You don't have to give it to me right now. But, before the end of the week if you could."

"Right — okay — thanks."

"Then there's the taxi fare. I thought you could get that, and I'll pay for the meal?"

That sounded fair — after all, the restaurants in the West End would be very expensive.

"I thought we'd go to McDonalds," he said.

"McDonalds?"

"Yes, there's one on the square, right next to the cinema where the premiere is being held."

"Sit in McDonalds — in this outfit?"

"We could always get takeout."

Just my luck, there wasn't a free seat to be had anywhere on the train. In the end, I had no choice but to spend the whole journey sitting across from Mr Ivers.

"I thought it would be interesting for us to look at all the films which Rick Ryland has made." Mr Ivers took out a few sheets of paper. "So, I put together a short report from my journals. Perhaps we could talk through them, and give marks out of ten?"

"Sorry, I have a bit of a headache. I thought I might close my eyes for a while."

"Oh. Okay then." Disappointment was etched on his face.

I didn't sleep a wink. Nor did I open my eyes again until the announcement came over the speakers that we were pulling into London.

***

If Mr Ivers' idea of dining out was McDonalds, there was no way I was going to fork out for a taxi. We took the Tube instead. Big mistake! I'd never seen so many people squashed together in such a confined space.

"Hey, do you mind? Watch the dress!" I shouted at the man leaning against me.

"What are you wearing that thing for, darlin'? You

going to a premiere or something?"

After around fifteen minutes, but what felt like ten days, we arrived at our destination. The day was turning into an unqualified disaster, but it would all be worth it in the end — when I got to see Rick.

True to his word, Mr Ivers bought us takeout from McDonalds. I refused the tomato sauce — it was way too risky in that dress.

By seven o'clock, a crowd had formed behind the barriers.

Pah! Peasants!

Mr Ivers and I strode down the red carpet as though we owned the place. I nodded to the people on my left and right. They probably thought I was one of the stars of the movie. Half way down the carpet, Mr Ivers tripped over his own feet. I gallantly pretended I wasn't with him, and carried on walking. He eventually caught up with me at the cinema doors.

"Tickets, please."

Mr Ivers was desperately searching his pockets while I smiled nervously at the stony-faced doorman.

"I could have sworn I put them in the inside pocket. Or maybe it was this one. Or maybe I took them out and put them on the table?"

No — please no. I was going to kill him.

"Oh, here they are." He held the tickets aloft.

Phew!

We made our way inside. The interior of the cinema was luxurious, and had been fitted out with all sorts of promotional décor for the premiere. There was even a life-size cut-out of Rick Ryland. I sidled over to it. We made a nice couple.

"Mr Ivers, would you take a photo?"

"Of you and the cardboard cut-out?"

"Of me and Rick. Yes, please. Take a couple; just in case."

After he'd taken the photograph, I ambled around the foyer, on the lookout for anyone famous. After about an hour, the noise levels outside increased dramatically.

"He's here," I said. "Rick's here." I pushed my way to the front to get a better view. He had a beautiful woman on his arm. What was *she* doing with him? Just then, I felt the strangest sensation. Something seemed to be pulling me back, but then whatever it was, suddenly released me, and I fell forward.

After I'd scrambled back to my feet, I could feel a draught on my bottom. I glanced around to find my dress had caught on something, and had ripped open at the back. Oh no! I was flashing my panties. Luckily, no one had noticed my mishap—yet!

I had to get out of there.

I cast the 'shrink' spell, and dashed back towards the entrance, dodging all the giant feet. Once outside, I ran around the side of the cinema and reversed the spell. What was I supposed to do? I couldn't go back inside with my backside hanging out of my dress—I'd be arrested.

Hold on! What was I thinking? I could use the 'take it back' spell. Why hadn't I thought of that earlier? I could have stayed in the cinema with Rick. Still, if I was quick, I might be able to get back inside. I cast the spell, and sure enough, my dress was as good as new. Thank goodness! I charged back around to the front of the cinema. The doors were now closed.

"Ticket please, madam." The doorman blocked my path.

"I've already been in. I came out just now."

"I didn't see you."

"That's because I was—err—never mind. Can't you just take my word for it?"

"Where's your ticket?"

"Inside. The man who I came with has it."

"Sorry, madam. No ticket, no entry. Please move away from the doors."

"But I want to see the film."

"Not happening."

I spent the next two and a half hours in a pub, a burger bar, and then wandering the streets of London. My hair was soaked, and my make-up had started to run. By the time I returned to the cinema, people were just starting to leave.

"Jill!" Mr Ivers said. "Where did you go? You were there one moment, and then—"

"I wasn't feeling very well."

"Oh dear. You missed a really good film."

"I just want to go home."

"You'll never guess what happened—"

"What?"

"Rick Ryland sat in the seat right in front of me!"

No! No, it couldn't be true. Life was so unfair.

***

"Morning, Jill," Mrs V said.

"Morning."

"How did it go last night?"

"Err—okay." I really did not want to relive that nightmare. "Look, I'm kind of busy. I'll catch up with you later."

Winky was on my desk.

"So, if it isn't the Hollywood starlet," he said.

"Shut it, you. I'm not in the mood."

"Really? I thought you'd be full of the joys of spring. Didn't Rick Ryland ask you to run away with him to Hollywood?"

"If you want any food today, you'll shut up about Rick Ryland right now."

"How about the movie? Was that any good?"

"Yes. I enjoyed it."

"Really? Because I didn't think you actually got to see it."

"Of course I did. Why do you think I went all the way down to London?"

"Because you had some insane notion that Rick Ryland would fall madly in love with you."

"Don't be ridiculous. Do you think I'm a child?"

"So you enjoyed the movie, then?"

"Yes, why do you keep asking me that?"

"Maybe because of this—" He pointed to the computer screen.

"What is it? I don't have time for your nonsense. I'm busy."

"I think you'll want to see this."

"Hurry up then." I sighed.

He clicked on the mouse and a video started to play. It looked as though it had been recorded on a mobile phone because the quality wasn't great. It appeared to have been taken by someone standing in the crowd at the premiere. It was focussed on the red carpet where Rick Ryland was waving to the crowd as he entered the cinema. He had that horrible woman, whoever she was, on his arm.

"Why are you showing me this? I was there, remember?"

"Keep watching," Winky said. "That's not the part I wanted you to see."

"I am rather busy."

Nothing much happened on screen for a few minutes, but then a familiar figure appeared from the right. No wonder it was familiar—it was me! I was at the cinema doors, trying to persuade the doorman to let me back in.

"So, you enjoyed the movie then?"

"Shut up. I've got work to do. Go and play with your helicopter."

I couldn't actually focus on work, but I kept shuffling papers around my desk, so Winky wouldn't keep interrupting me.

The phone rang; it was Colonel Briggs.

"Morning, Jill. How are you this beautiful morning?"

"Very well, Colonel, thanks," I lied.

"That's good. Look, I know you're busy, but I just wanted to check whether you'd made any progress at all with Sir Cuthbert's case?"

"Nothing much to report, I'm afraid, but I'm still on it. I promise I'll call you the moment I have anything."

"Okay, Jill, I know you'll do your best. Thanks a lot. Bye."

"Bye, Colonel."

I felt bad that I had nothing more to tell him. I really

should have been working on the case instead of moping around, feeling sorry for myself. I dug out the file, and started going back through my interviews. I also took another look at the photo which Sir Cuthbert had given me of the missing vase.

That's when I spotted it.

Chapter 11

"Barry isn't very happy," Pearl said.

"What's wrong with him now?" Why couldn't I have at least one pet who didn't cause me grief all the time?

"You'd better go and talk to him." Amber pointed up the stairs.

Barry had his head resting on his front paws; he looked very sorry for himself.

"What's wrong, Barry?"

"You won't let me have a pet."

"I'm just not sure it's a good idea for a dog to have a hamster as a pet."

"I know lots of dogs who have them."

"Name me one."

"There's Peter, and Stewart, and Agnes. Then there's Ivan. Even Chief's got one—"

"Chief? You mean Drake's dog?"

"Yeah. He told me he has one."

"Are you sure? You're not just making this up?"

"No. You can ask Drake; he'll tell you."

"Okay, here's what we'll do. Let's go to the pet shop and speak to the owner to see if he thinks it's a good idea."

"Okay. Can we go now? Let's go now. Can we, please? I want to go now."

"Yes, okay, okay."

Sheesh! My life wasn't my own.

Rupert's Pets was just off the market square. As we got closer to the shop, I struggled to keep hold of Barry as he became more and more excited. Hopefully, once we'd spoken to the owner, and he'd confirmed that it wasn't a good idea, Barry would forget the whole thing.

The sign on the door read: *'Dogs welcome'*, so I took Barry inside, trying desperately to keep him in check.

The man behind the counter beamed at us. "Hello, you two, and welcome to Rupert's Pets!"

"Are you Rupert?"

"Rupert's on holiday. I'm Eddie. How can I help you?"

"I realise this is a silly question," I said in a low voice, trying not to let Barry hear. "But would you please confirm that it isn't a good idea for a dog to have a pet hamster."

"There's absolutely no reason why a dog shouldn't have a hamster as a pet. In fact, I'd go as far as to say that dogs make excellent owners."

"Are you serious?"

"Of course. It will keep your dog—what's his name?"

"Barry."

"It will keep Barry amused for hours, and I'm sure he'll make a very good owner. What do you say, boy? Would you like a hamster?"

"Yes, please. I'd love a hamster. Can I have a hamster?" Barry jumped up and down, and pirouetted with excitement. "I want a hamster."

So much for that plan.

It came to seventy-five pounds in total. The hamster had cost only five pounds, but then there was the cage, and the extension to the cage, and the food, and the toys—including a mirror. I'd always thought it was only budgies and parrots that had mirrors, but it turned out that hamsters were partial to them too. They're particularly vain according to Eddie.

Seventy-five pounds! Like I didn't already have enough money problems!

Back at the flat, Barry couldn't have been any happier. He sat watching his new little friend running round and round on his wheel.

"Are you happy now, Barry?"

"Yes, thank you. I love Hammy."

"Is that what you're going to call him? Hammy the hamster?"

"He already had his name: Hamlet."

"Hamlet the hamster? Right. Well, I'll leave you and Hammy to get to know one another."

"Say goodbye to Jill, Hammy," Barry said.

"Goodbye, Jill." The hamster jumped off his wheel.

"You can talk?"

"Of course I can. Oh, and by the way, I prefer Hamlet."

"Oh—okay. Bye then, Hamlet."

"Goodbye, Jill."

So now I had not just two, but three crazy animals: Winky, the psycho cat, Barry, the big soft dog, and now Hamlet, the hamster. Surely, my life couldn't get any crazier.

***

I ran into Luther Stone on my way back to the flat.

"Busy day, Jill?"

"So-so. How about you?"

"Oh, you know. The usual: profit and loss, balance sheets, that sort of thing. Not very exciting. Not like your job. Being a private investigator must be really interesting."

"Yeah, most of the time."

"By the way, do you remember I mentioned the new brochure I'm having done?"

"Brochure?" It was engraved on my heart. "Err? Oh, yes. I remember now."

"I wondered if maybe you had a few minutes now? I thought I could take a photo and do a quick interview. Only if you have the time, of course."

"Yeah, absolutely." Maybe I'd written Luther off too quickly. He seemed rather keen to get me over to his place. Primarily to do the brochure, obviously. But who knew where it might lead? Steady on, Jill, don't get carried away. Remember what happened last time.

I followed him to his flat. He'd stripped all the carpets out, and replaced them with wooden flooring. It looked great, but I could barely keep my feet. I had to hold onto the furniture to prevent myself from slipping.

"Are you alright, Jill?"

"Fine, yeah."

I'd never seen so much chrome. I daren't touch anything for fear of leaving fingerprints. "You have a lot of chrome."

"That's my brother. He works at Chrome City. You must have seen it?"

"No, I don't think so."

"It's just off the high street. Everything they sell has a chrome finish. He did me a good deal, so I didn't like to say no. It's terrible to keep clean though. Come this way. I've set us up in here."

We went through to what I assumed was the spare bedroom. It contained only a single armchair.

"Would you like to take a seat, and I'll take a quick snap? All very informal; nothing to worry about."

"Should I do something with my hair, first?"

"It looks fine to me."

"Maybe I ought to fix my make-up?"

"No, honestly you look absolutely fine."

"Okay." I sat in the armchair, and tried to look as alluring as possible.

"Are you feeling okay?" He looked concerned. "You look in pain."

So much for *alluring*.

"I'm fine."

"Let's try again."

"Okay." I went for sultry this time.

"Are you sure you're okay? Would you like a glass of water?"

"Yes. Really, I'm fine."

"Just look at the camera, relax and be as natural as you can."

Natural? How was I supposed to do that? I stared into the camera lens, and tried to smile.

"Maybe don't try so hard, Jill?"

"Okay, sorry." I tried again.

"That's better. Great. Now, if we could do a short interview. Just one or two quotes which I can place next to your photo in the brochure."

"Of course, yes."

"I realise that I haven't been your accountant for very long, but could you tell me what you think about the service you've received so far?"

"Your service has been absolutely excellent, Luther. It's been beyond words. I've just loved every second of it."

"I was thinking more about the accuracy of the reporting, and the timeliness?"

"Right, yes, of course. The accuracy and the timeliness has been fantastic, and you have been nothing less than wonderful, Luther."

"Right, well I think I have everything I need there. Thank you for that, Jill."

"Is that it? Because there are other complimentary things I could say."

"No, really. I think I have all the quotes I need. I'm sorry to have delayed you."

No dinner? No drinks?

"Bye, Jill. Thanks again."

"Bye, Luther."

I was back in the corridor when a voice came from behind me.

"So!" said Betty. "That's your game is it? You were trying to put me off Luther, so you could keep him for yourself."

"No, Betty. You've got it all wrong."

"I saw you! Don't lie to me. I thought you were my friend, Jill. I thought I could trust you."

"But, Betty, I was only having photos taken—"

"Photos? What kind of photos? Don't tell me—I can guess. How could you?"

With that, she stormed off.

***

Grandma had summoned me to Ever A Wool Moment. Kathy was behind the counter when I walked through the door.

"Where is she?"

"In campaign HQ at the back. Good luck."

"Is she in a good mood?"

Kathy laughed. "As always."

"Grandma, you wanted to see—"

"Sit down, Jill."

"I am quite busy at the—"

"Be quiet, girl. Whatever you're doing obviously isn't as important as this. I thought we should have a strategy meeting for my election campaign."

What was it with strategy meetings all of a sudden?

"I'm not sure I'm the best person for this job."

"I've told you—it's already decided. You will head my campaign. There's only one other candidate, and that's Mr Boyle. Do you know him?"

"No. I don't think so."

"Lance."

"Lance Boyle?"

"That's right."

Somehow, I managed not to laugh. This was obviously a serious matter.

"The polls show we're neck and neck at the moment," Grandma said. "So we have to find something which will give us an advantage."

"Perhaps we could talk through your policies, and then I could—"

"No, no, none of that nonsense. That won't do any good. I need you to dig up the dirt on Lance."

"Hold on. Are you talking about running a dirty

campaign? A smear campaign?"

"Of course."

"But that's not ethical."

"Jill, dear, you have a lot to learn about politics. No one ever won an election by being ethical."

"I'm sorry, but I'm not prepared to do anything underhand."

"I think you'll find you are. Why do you think I asked you to do this? Because of your experience spearheading an election campaign?" She laughed. "Of course not, but who better to dig the dirt on someone than a private investigator?"

So *that's* why she'd asked me. I should have known. "But that's not what I do in my job. I try to help people."

"Yeah, yeah. Very interesting I'm sure. Now listen—I want you to find out all you can about Lance Boyle. If he has any dark secrets, I want you to uncover them, and then we can 'leak' them to the press."

"What if he doesn't have any?"

"Then, we'll make some up."

"That's despicable."

"I know. Brilliant, isn't it?"

It was pointless arguing with Grandma, so I let her think I'd go along with her plan. But there was no way I was going to run a smear campaign. Unlike her, I had morals. What? Of course I do—at least when it suits me. My best bet was to contact my counterpart, Lance Boyle's campaign manager. Surely we could reach a gentlemen's agreement that we'd both run a clean campaign. That would ensure a fair election, and let the best candidate win.

***

Terry Brown certainly didn't act like a guilty man. When I'd contacted him to ask if I could talk to him again, he'd raised no objection, and when I arrived at the house he was most welcoming.

"Come in. Have a seat."

"I need to ask you about one of the items in your collection."

"Which one?"

"The plate with the serpent on it."

"Beautiful isn't it? It's one of my recent acquisitions; I only bought it a couple of weeks ago."

"It's lovely." I took out the photograph which Sir Cuthbert had given me. "Would you mind taking a look at this? Do you recognise anything?"

"Is that the vase which was stolen?"

"It is, but do you see anything else you recognise? In the background?"

Terry looked a little closer. "That's my plate." He tapped the photo with his finger. "I had no idea it used to belong to Sir Cuthbert."

"Surely you must have seen it in the house?"

"I spend most of my time in the kitchen. The only time I go into the house is when Lady Phoebe wants to discuss menus with me."

"Could I ask how you acquired it?"

"I buy most of my pieces from the same two or three shops. That particular item I bought from Antony's Antiques."

"Where's that?"

"In Winminster, about fifty miles from Washbridge."

"Do you mind if I ask how much you paid for it?"

"Not at all. It was just over three thousand pounds."

"Thank you very much for your help. I'll be in touch."

"What about the plate?" Terry said. "Was it stolen too? If so, I have to return it to Sir Cuthbert."

"Hold on to it for now. I'll be in touch when I know more."

Chapter 12

I'd no sooner got back to my flat than there was a knock on the door. I didn't want to see Betty again because she was obviously annoyed at me, and I definitely didn't want to see Mr Ivers. I'd had enough of him to last me a lifetime. But what if it was Luther? I thought we'd hit it off rather well. I'd better check just in case.

"Kathy?"

"Gee, Jill. Don't look so pleased to see me."

"I wasn't expecting you."

"Which of your *many* men friends were you expecting?"

"I don't have *many* men friends."

"I suppose it all depends on your definition of *many*. In my book any more than one is many."

"Did you want something?"

"To be *invited in* would be a good start."

"Sorry, come on in. Would you like a cup of tea?"

"That would be great, and a few custard creams wouldn't go amiss."

I made tea for us both, and we settled down in the living room.

"So what brings you here?"

"I actually came to have a moan about your grandmother."

"I did warn you that going to work at 'Ever' was a bad idea."

"I'm beginning to think you were right. I don't mind hard work, but she keeps coming up with all these new initiatives, and then leaves me to run them. And now, she's in the back office all the time, busy with her election campaign. I didn't even realise there was an election in

Washbridge."

"Why don't you tell her you want more money for all the additional responsibility?"

"I did."

"What did she say?"

"She laughed at me."

"You could always threaten to resign."

"I don't want to quit. I like the job, and the money's okay. It's just that she drives me mad."

"Welcome to my world."

We spent the next half an hour pulling Grandma to pieces, and talking about all the things we'd like to do to her.

"There's an arts and crafts show next week," Kathy said. "Lizzie's going to take some of her beanies."

"Please don't tell me she's taking the Frankenstein ones."

"They're hybrids. They show a vivid imagination."

"They show a warped mind, if you ask me."

"We're not sure which one to enter: the donguin or the kangadillo."

"Why don't you teach Lizzie to knit? She could make a scarf or a hat. That would be a nice thing to enter into the competition. People will think there's something wrong with her when they see those beanies."

"I'd rather she had a vivid imagination than be so uptight that she spent all of her time cataloguing them, and arranging them in alphabetical order, like you used to do."

Kathy stared at the empty plate. "Are there any more custard creams?"

"No, sorry," I lied. "Those were the last ones."

I thought Kathy would never go. What? Of course, I loved her, but that didn't mean I wasn't pleased to see the back of her sometimes. And besides, I was desperate for a custard cream. I'd kept three hidden in the Tupperware box because Kathy would have scoffed the lot.

I'd just taken the box out when there was another knock at the door. Oh, no! Had she forgotten something? I quickly slid the custard creams under the sofa.

No one was there; the corridor was deserted. I stepped outside. "Ouch!" What the—? Something had stung my bare foot. I looked down, and there on the carpet was some kind of slimy creature.

A jellyfish!

Someone had put a jellyfish on the floor, right outside my front door. And I knew who. There was only one person in the building who had an unhealthy obsession with sea creatures, and that was Betty Longbottom. The evil little fiend! This had to be her idea of revenge because she'd seen me come out of Luther's flat. It was hardly *my* fault that Luther found me irresistible. She should get back with Norman; he was perfect for her.

Ouch! It really stung. Just wait until I saw Betty again; I'd have a few choice words to say to her. Now, how do you treat a jellyfish sting? I'd better go check on Google.

What? No! Surely that couldn't be right.

***

Mrs V looked perplexed when I arrived at the office. "What's wrong?" I said.

"I'm sorry, Jill. I did tell them they should wait until you arrived, but—"

"Who's *they*? What's going on?"

"I don't really know. It's all very strange. Perhaps you should take a look."

I could just about squeeze through the door. My office was full of equipment. There were lighting stands, reflective screens, and a tripod with a camera on it. The photographer and his assistants had all their attention focussed towards the leather sofa where Winky was sitting.

"What's going on?" I shouted.

The photographer turned to me. "Do you mind?"

"Pardon me, I'm *so* sorry. Who *are* you, exactly?"

"I'm Dartagnan."

"Ha, ha. Very funny. Now, what's your real name?"

"That *is* my *real* name."

"And are these two the other musketeers?"

"Huh?" He looked confused.

"Dartagnan—musketeers?" No? Just me then.

"This is Elizabeth and Eliza, my two assistants. We're here to photograph Winky."

"But why?"

"I've been commissioned to work on the new Children's Eye Patches catalogue, and Winky has been kind enough to offer to model a new range which has been specifically designed for the pet section."

"*Is there* a pet section in the Children's Eye Patches catalogue?"

"There will be, and that's mainly down to Winky. I understand from the owners of the company that other cats have seen Winky on FelineSocial, and as a result, that side of the business is now booming. That's why they plan to launch a new catalogue, with an additional section, specifically for pets. And Winky has kindly agreed to model the new range."

"When you say he's agreed to do it? How exactly did he do that? He's a cat."

"I believe it was all arranged by email. With his owner, I assume."

Winky had been at my computer again.

"Is he getting paid?"

"Err—well, that's nothing to do with me. That's between him and the owners of Children's Eye Patches."

"I only ask because I am his agent."

Winky gave me a look.

"I negotiate all his contracts: book sales, film rights, modelling eye patches—"

"Sorry, I didn't realise. Well, as I said, you'll have to take it up with the owners of the company."

"Trust me, I will. I have to look after the interests of my client."

I spent the next fifty minutes watching Winky modelling a number of eye patches. Some of them were quite fetching. I particularly liked the red and black striped limited edition.

***

The nearest car park to Antony's Antiques was about a quarter of a mile away, but it was a beautiful day and I wasn't in a hurry. I hadn't walked far when I heard a commotion. A cat came sprinting around the corner, closely followed by four dogs. The poor thing looked terrified. I watched it run down an alleyway with the dogs in hot pursuit. I followed and saw that it had come to a halt with its back to a wall. The alleyway was a dead end, and the walls were way too high for it to jump over. It was well and truly cornered. The pack of dogs was moving towards it—barking, teeth bared. The cat's fur was on end; its tail raised. It was spitting at the dogs, but I could tell by the look in its eyes that it was terrified. Any second now, one of the dogs would pounce, and then they'd all attack. I glanced around to make sure there was no one around, and then cast the 'illusion' spell. Suddenly the dogs stopped in their tracks, and instead of barking, they began to whimper, as they slowly backed away. When one of them turned tail and ran, the others followed. They'd all seen a lion roaring at them.

The cat looked stunned.

"Here pussy, pussy, pussy." I put my hand out to stroke it, but it scratched me, and ran away. Charming, but then if anyone should know better than to expect gratitude from a cat, it should be me.

Antony's Antiques was a small shop in a street full of similar shops. This was apparently Winminster's antiques quarter. As I walked through the door, a bell rang, and a funny little man with long grey hair in a ponytail came scuttling out.

"Good morning. How can I help you?"
"Are you Antony?"
"I prefer Tony."
"Oh right. It's just that the sign says—"

"Ah yes. My partner's name is Ann, Ann Jessop. We combined our names: Ann and Tony to make Antony. See?"

"Err—yeah." Clear as mud.

"So, how can I help you, young lady?"

"My name is Jill Gooder. I'm a private investigator. I'm looking into the theft of a vase from the home of Sir Cuthbert Cutts."

"Oh yes. I know Sir Cuthbert and his wife, Lady Phoebe."

"May I show you a picture of the vase?"

"Certainly, but I must stress that we are very careful about checking the provenance of all the items we sell."

I showed him the photo.

"I haven't seen anything like that."

"What about the item in the background?"

"The plate? Yes, I do recognise that. In fact, I sold it to one of the employees from the Hall. Terry Brown, the chef."

"Can you tell me how you came by it?"

"Of course. It was sold to me by Lady Phoebe herself."

Something very strange was going on here.

***

It was tambourine day at Coffee Triangle. It had been ages since I'd shaken one, so I thought *why the heck not*? I'd treated myself to a latte and a blueberry muffin. What? I had to keep my strength up; it took a lot of energy to shake a tambourine. Although I say so myself, I had been one of the better tambourine players at school, and I still had the knack. I'd just finished shaking it when I heard a familiar voice. Jack Maxwell? What was he doing here? I peeked around the side of the booth, and there he was. I was about to go over and join him for a tambourine duet when I realised he was with someone. A very attractive redhead. Before I could duck back out of sight, he spotted me, and came over.

"Hi, Jill. Are you here for a quick shake of a tambourine?"

"Tambourine? I had no idea they even did that sort of thing," I lied. "It all seems a little silly. I just came in for a coffee."

"It's great fun. You should come here on a Friday. It's drum day."

"I don't think so. I've heard quite enough drumming lately from my nephew, Mikey. Look, I don't want to keep you, Jack. I can see you're with *someone*," I said, pointedly.

"That's Deirdre. She's the paranormal consultant I told you about."

"The one that you didn't want to waste your time on?"

"I did say that, didn't I? To be honest, I'm becoming a bit of a convert. Deirdre isn't your normal run-of-the-mill paranormal consultant."

"Why? Because she's attractive, and has big boobs?" Had I really said that out loud?

"How shallow do you think I am?"

"You're a man—of course you're shallow."

"If you must know, Deirdre and I were discussing dancing."

I laughed. "Is that what you call it?"

"It's true. We share a common interest in dance."

"You mean you like to boogie?"

"Not that kind of dancing. Ballroom dancing. You

know: waltz, quickstep, foxtrot, that kind of thing."

"You? Ballroom dance?"

"Sure. Why not? I actually have medals for it, and it turns out so does Deirdre."

"Me too," I lied.

"Really?"

"Heck yes. Dozens of them. I've lost count." Before he could press me for details, I figured I should steer the subject away from dancing. "So? You buy into this paranormal mumbo jumbo now, do you?"

"More than I did. I guess that's down to Deirdre. She's brought a very scientific approach to bear on the investigation."

"I just bet she has."

"You shouldn't scoff. Just because you don't understand something, it doesn't mean it isn't real."

"You've changed your tune!"

"That's down to Deirdre. She's made me see there's more to this world than we can see, hear or smell."

"Smells fishy to me," I said under my breath.

"What?"

"Nothing. I'm very pleased for the two of you. I'm sure you be very happy together. Anyway, I have to go. I have cases which aren't going to solve themselves."

I watched him walk back over to Deirdre. What? Of course I wasn't jealous. Jack and I were just friends. He could see whoever he wanted. If he chose to waste his time on a redheaded bimbo with big boobs, that was his business. I was totally cool with it. Totally.

Chapter 13

I had a meeting arranged with Sir Monty and Lady Bunty who were close friends of Sir Cuthbert and Lady Phoebe. According to Sir Cuthbert, their knowledge of the local antiques trade might prove useful.

Their house, which was a few miles to the north of Washbridge, was surrounded by extensive grounds through which ran a narrow road. I left my car around the back of the house in what was clearly the staff car park. The cars parked there were in stark contrast to those on the front where I'd spotted a Rolls Royce, a Bentley and several sports cars. I understood, from what Sir Cuthbert had told me, that Sir Monty was something of a collector of cars.

I was greeted at the door by a butler, who told me his name was Arbuthnot, but that I should call him 'Not'.

"This way, madam," he said. "Sir Monty and Lady Bunty are expecting you. They're in the green room."

"Thank you, Not." Huh?

He led the way up a grand staircase, and along a corridor resplendent with paintings and tapestries.

"Here we are, madam."

I was a little confused because the green room turned out to be predominantly purple.

"Miss Gooder!" A short, elderly man with a monocle and a walking stick, hobbled towards me. Behind him, seated on a chaise longue, was an elderly lady dressed in what I can only describe as lots of feathers. I assumed it was some sort of housecoat, but the overall effect was that she looked like she'd been swallowed by an ostrich.

"Pleased to meet you, Sir Monty," I said.

"Likewise, my dear. Sir Cuthbert said you'd be calling. This is my wife, Lady Bunty."

The ostrich got up and came over to shake my hand.

"Now," Sir Monty said. "Before we start, would you like a glass of sherry?"

"Could I possibly have a cup of coffee instead, please?"

"Of course. Milk and sugar?"

"Milk and one sugar, please." I thought it best not to confuse him with fractions.

'Not' was despatched to fetch the drinks.

The elderly couple were charming. Sir Monty was as mad as a box of frogs, and Lady Bunty was only a couple of tadpoles behind him. But they knew their antiques, and seemed to be familiar with the pieces owned by Sir Cuthbert and Lady Phoebe.

"Have you had anything go missing yourselves?" I asked. "Any break-ins?"

"No, nothing like that," Lady Bunty said. "We have a very good security system here. I'm rather surprised that Cuthbert has had this problem. I assume it's an inside job."

"We're not sure at the moment. Do you often socialise with Sir Cuthbert and Lady Phoebe?"

"I wouldn't say 'often'. We see them about twice a year. No more than that. But then we did see —"

"Bunty!" Sir Monty snapped.

At that precise moment, we were interrupted by the return of 'Not' with my coffee.

"Please go on, Lady Bunty," I said. "If you think it

would help?"

"She really shouldn't have said anything," Sir Monty said. "I hope we can rely on your discretion?"

"Of course. Anything you tell me will be treated in the strictest confidence."

"Bunty and I went to Ascot for Ladies Day. On our way back home, we stopped off at one of our favourite restaurants, the Tudor Fox in Winminster. Do you know it?"

I shook my head—it was probably way above my pay grade.

"As we were making our way from the car park, we spotted Phoebe Cutts coming out of an antique shop."

"Yes." Bunty picked up the story. "I was just about to call to her when I realised—" She hesitated. "She wasn't with Sir Cuthbert. She was with a much younger man. He'd been waiting outside the shop for her."

"The man looked a bit of a scoundrel to me," Sir Monty chimed in. "Never trust a man who drives a Porsche—that's what I always say."

"A Porsche? What colour was it?"

"A horrible shade of green."

***

I'd arranged to meet Lance Boyle's campaign manager at Cuppy C. His name was Dexter Long, and he said I'd recognise him because he'd be wearing a blue and white rosette. He'd presumably mentioned the colour just in case I got him mixed up with the many other rosette-wearing customers.

I spotted him at the corner table.

"Hi, Jill," Amber said. "Drink?"

"I've actually got a meeting with that guy over there. Would you bring a latte and a blueberry muffin over to me?"

"Did you ought to be eating blueberry muffins?"

"I'll just have a small one."

"We only have the one size—I wouldn't call it small."

"I would. Thanks."

The man with the rosette stood up as I approached.

"Dexter Long?"

"Please call me Dexy. Everyone does."

"Right, Dexy it is then."

"Have a seat, Jill. I understand you're the campaign manager for Mirabel Millbright?"

"That's right. She's my grandmother. I was 'volunteered' into the job."

"Oh dear! It's a cut and thrust business, you know. I hope you're prepared for it. I'm run off my feet, and I'm up until gone midnight most days, working on the campaign."

"There you go, Jill," Amber said, placing the coffee and muffin in front of me.

"Thanks, Amber."

"That looks delicious." Dexter was practically salivating at the sight of my muffin.

"Would you like one?"

"No thanks, I'm watching my waistline. I generally stick to plain biscuits."

"Me too."

"The reason I asked you to meet me, Dexter—err—Dexy—is because I want to ensure that the election is a clean one. I don't want to get involved with dirty tricks or smear campaigns."

"I'm so very pleased to hear you say that, Jill. It makes a refreshing change. I've been involved with many a campaign, and I have to tell you that the lengths some people will go to in order to win, is quite unbelievable, and totally unacceptable. My candidate, Lance Boyle, is an upstanding citizen, and he is only interested in fighting this campaign on the issues and his policies. He doesn't want it to become personal, and neither do I. I wouldn't want to represent anyone who would get involved with underhand tactics."

"Really?" I breathed a sigh of relief. "I was a little worried that you would laugh at me for suggesting we try and run a clean campaign."

"Not at all. I'm pleased you contacted me. You can rest assured that there will be no dirty tricks from our side."

"That's great."

After a few minutes, Dexy had to rush off, so Amber and Pearl came over to join me.

"Were you on a date, Jill?" Pearl said.

"No, I'm not dating anyone at the moment."

"Hmm," said Amber. "For someone who's not dating anyone, you seem to have a lot of names in your little black book."

"I don't have a *little black book* either. If you must know, that was Dexter 'Dexy' Long. He's the campaign manager for Lance Boyle, who is Grandma's opponent in the local election. I've reached an agreement with him that there will be no dirty tricks."

Amber laughed. "You are kidding, aren't you?"

"What do you mean?"

"Grandma, not employ dirty tricks? That'll be a first."

"It doesn't matter what Grandma wants to do. I'm the campaign manager, and I won't countenance any dirty tricks."

"Good luck with that," Pearl said.

"You'll see. I'm going to run a clean campaign, and we'll still win."

The girls looked unconvinced, but I'd show them.

***

"You're wonderfully naïve," Grandma said when I caught up with her in the back office at 'Ever'.

"What do you mean?"

"Do you actually believe that the other candidate isn't going to resort to dirty tricks?"

"I've spoken to his campaign manager. He seems like a decent chap."

She laughed.

"Look, I'm a pretty good judge of character, and I trust him."

Grandma was shaking her head, but I ignored her.

"Wouldn't you rather be elected after running a clean campaign, than have to resort to dirty tricks and smear tactics?"

Grandma shrugged. "I don't care either way, as long as I win."

"Well I do. My reputation is on the line here."

"Look, young lady, you'd better know what you're doing. If this campaign fails to get me elected, it will be your fault."

"I'm confident that we'll win," I said, feeling anything but.

"You'd better be right." She gave me a look that chilled me to the bones. "Anyway, I've been thinking. Seeing as you're going to be heavily involved with my election campaign, I don't want you to have any other distractions, so I've decided there won't be any magic lessons for a while."

Hurrah! "Oh dear, that's disappointing."

"You look *really* disappointed. And there's something else." She hesitated. "I've decided to move you up to level three."

"What?" I gasped. "Already?"

"That's what I said."

"Do you think I'm ready?"

"We can pretend you are. You'll just have to fake it 'til you make it."

"Thanks. I don't know what to say."

"There's no time for all that. You should be out campaigning and stuff. Why are you sitting here talking to me?"

"Right, okay. Thanks, Grandma. Bye."

***

I was really excited about being made a level three witch. I wanted to tell someone, but I could hardly share my news with Kathy or Mrs V, so I magicked myself back to Candlefield to see the twins at Cuppy C. But then, just as I was about to walk into the tea room, I had a moment's self-doubt. How would they take it? They were still on level two. How would they feel when I told them that I had now moved ahead of them? Would they resent me? I'd soon find out.

Cuppy C, was deserted, and it wasn't difficult to see why.

"Girls?" I shouted to the twins, who were busy doing something behind the counter.

"Sorry, Jill. Can't talk—we've got a chocolate fountain emergency," Pearl shouted, without looking up.

"So I see." The floor was covered in chocolate, and there were footprints where people had paddled through it.

"What happened?"

"It's this stupid chocolate fountain," Amber said. "It suddenly went crazy and started producing ten times more chocolate than it should. It's gone everywhere: onto the counter, onto the floor—everywhere. We're flooded in chocolate!"

"Can't you just switch it off?"

"Gee thanks, Jill. We would never have thought of that," Pearl said, and turned to her sister. "Duh! Amber, we should just switch it off."

"Thanks, Jill," Amber said. "That's genius!"

"Sorry, I just thought—"

"We've tried everything. We've even turned the power off. But the chocolate just keeps pouring out. We can't stop it."

"Can I try?"

"What can you do?"

"I don't know, but maybe I'll be able to think of something."

"Knock yourself out," Amber said.

I took off my shoes, and paddled through the chocolate to the counter.

"Do you have the instruction manual?"

"What instruction manual?" Pearl said.

"It must have come with one, surely?"

"I think I put it in the drawer," Amber said.

"*Now* might be a good time to get it out."

She made her way over to the cupboard at the far side of the counter, and returned holding a small booklet. "There you go."

I flicked through all the usual set up instructions, and the 'how to get started' section. Then I came to a section headed '*What to do if your chocolate fountain floods your premises*'.

"I think I might have found the relevant section," I said, but the girls were too busy pressing buttons, and pulling levers to take any notice.

I read it through again just to be sure.

"Stand back, girls. I've got this."

They looked at me sceptically, but did as I said. I cast the relevant spell, and instantly, the chocolate stopped flowing.

"Wow, Jill! How did you do that?" Amber looked gobsmacked.

"R T B M!"

"What?"

"Read The Blooming Manual!"

I thought it was R T—"

"Never mind that. It's fixed—that's all that matters."

"What was the problem?"

"You had a chocolate goblin in there."

"A what?"

"Look, here." I pointed to the manual. "It says: 'If the fountain starts to produce too much chocolate, and it is impossible to stop it, this is an indication that a chocolate goblin has taken possession of your machine. You have to use an 'anti-goblin' spell which gets rid of the goblin, and restores the fountain to proper working order.' If you'd read the manual, you would have known that. Duh!"

"Thanks, Jill," Amber said. "You're a life saver."

"Yeah, but look at the state of this place." Pearl pointed to the floor. "I think we should get rid of this stupid machine."

"Me too. I never did like it anyway," Amber agreed.

"I'll give you a hand cleaning up." I took off my jacket, and hung it on the back of a chair.

"Thanks, Jill. By the way, did you come over for any particular reason?"

"I did, actually. There's something I have to tell the two of you, and I hope you aren't going to be too mad at me."

"After you just saved us from being drowned in chocolate? I don't think so."

"Grandma just made me a level three witch."

The two girls stared, wide-eyed, and I was unsure how they'd taken it.

"That's fantastic!" Amber was all smiles.

"Yeah, absolutely brilliant!" Pearl nodded.

"Yes, you deserve it, Jill, for getting rid of the goblin," Amber said.

"So you don't mind?"

"Of course we don't mind!" Pearl said. "We're not bothered about moving up the levels. You know that. But you can go all the way. We're really thrilled for you."

"I just hope I can cope."

"You'll be fine."

"Come on then. Let's get this chocolate cleaned up."

Chapter 14

"Mum! Are you there, Mum?" I still felt a little self-conscious whenever I called my mother, even though I was alone in the flat, and no one could see me.

"Jill? Is everything okay?" She looked concerned.

"Yes, I'm fine."

"You had me worried."

"You don't have to worry every time I call you."

"I know, but I'm your mother. That's my job. I still feel guilty about taking your custard creams by the way."

"Don't worry about that. Look, I called you because Grandma has moved me up to level three."

"She has?"

"Didn't you know?"

"No. When did this happen?"

"Earlier today, and I'm not sure if I'm ready."

There was a long silence. My mother looked deep in thought.

"This is the point where you say 'of course you're ready'."

"Sorry. I'm sure you are."

"You're not doing a great job of convincing me, here. Do you think it's too early?"

"Grandma knows what she's doing, but—" She hesitated, and then forced a smile. "Never mind."

"Never mind 'never mind'. What were you going to say?"

"Just that I've never heard of any witch moving up to level three so quickly—ever."

"Maybe I should tell her to move me back down?"

"She won't do that. For all of her faults, Grandma *does*

know what she's doing. If she thinks you're ready, then you are."

"But I make such stupid mistakes."

"What do you mean?"

"Well, look at the time I was levitating over a wall, and I used the wrong option to descend. I dropped to the ground like a brick."

That brought a smile to my mother's face for some reason.

"Everyone makes mistakes when they're learning. That's nothing."

"It didn't feel like nothing at the time. It really hurt. And, that's not the only time I've messed up. Look what happened at your wedding."

"I didn't realise anything had."

"I haven't told anyone — it's kind of embarrassing."

"You have to tell me now that you've started."

"I didn't say anything at the time, but your wedding fell on the same day as Kathy's birthday. When you told me the date, I'd already arranged to spend the day with her."

"You ought to have said something."

"It shouldn't have mattered. If I'd had my brain in gear, I would have realised that I could have attended your wedding, and then gone back to Washbridge to spend the day with Kathy because time stands still when I'm in Candlefield."

"I'm guessing you didn't do that."

"I was such an idiot. I spent the whole day, flitting back and forth between the wedding and Kathy's birthday celebrations. It was a nightmare. By the time I'd done, I was exhausted."

"Oh, dear." My mother laughed.

"See what I mean? I'm an idiot!"

"Sorry, I shouldn't laugh." It took her a few seconds to compose herself again. "None of that matters. We all make mistakes. It's not like anyone is watching you. If you hadn't told me, no one would ever have known."

"But I feel like there's thousands of eyes watching everything I do—just waiting for me to make a mistake."

"Now you're starting to sound paranoid."

"I know. I'm sorry. It's just that the move up to the next level came out of the blue. I'm sure I'll be okay."

"You definitely will, and I'm sorry I laughed at your wedding mishap."

"That's okay. Even I can see the funny side now."

"You know you can always call me if you have any moments of self-doubt."

"I know, thanks. Actually, there is a favour I'd like to ask of you."

"Of course. Anything."

"This might sound a bit crazy, but—"

What was I doing? Why was I getting my mother involved?

"Jill?"

"Sorry, I'd zoned out. Do you remember Jack Maxwell?"

"The policeman? Are you and he an item?"

"No, I don't think so—maybe—I don't know. I have no idea what our relationship is. Or even if we have one."

"So how can I help?"

"I know it shouldn't bother me—"

"I feel a 'but' coming on."

"But, recently he's been working with a 'paranormal consultant'."

"A what?"

"Yeah, I know; that's what I thought. Apparently she can *see* ghosts. Or, at least, that's what she claims on her résumé. It's obviously nonsense, but she seems to have everyone fooled—including Jack."

"And would this paranormal consultant be attractive?"

"I hadn't really noticed. I suppose so. Possibly. I just thought that if she happened to see a *real* ghost, then just maybe—"

"It would scare her off?"

"Yeah. Something like that. Do you think I'm being horrible?"

"Yes."

"Will you do it anyway?"

"Of course. Anything for my darling daughter."

"That's great, Mum. Thanks."

***

I'd decided to take Barry for a walk, but when I checked upstairs at Cuppy C he wasn't there. There was a note from the twins saying they'd taken him to the park. I was about to make my way over to Aunt Lucy's when a little voice shouted.

"Excuse me."

I turned around, confused for a moment.

"Over here." It was the hamster calling to me.

"Oh, hello there."

"It's Jill, isn't it?"

"Yeah, that's me."

"Jill, I wondered if I could ask you a favour?"

"Sure, Hammy. What can I do for you?"

"Well, first of all, could I ask that you call me 'Hamlet', please?"

"I'm sorry. I thought you were okay with 'Hammy'."

"No, not really. That's what Barry insists on calling me. I have asked him to call me Hamlet, but it doesn't seem to register."

"Hamlet is an unusual name for a hamster."

"I chose it myself."

"Oh? Okay. So what is it I can do for you, Hammy — sorry — Hamlet?"

"It's rather delicate, and I'm not really sure how to put this, but well — err — Barry's a perfectly nice dog — but he's not exactly the full shilling, is he?"

"He is a bit—"

"Simple?"

"I was going to say 'naïve'."

"Our conversations aren't exactly what you'd call stimulating. They basically revolve around his love of going to the park and eating, which between you and me, are not the most interesting of topics. What I really need is something a little more intellectually challenging. So, I thought maybe a few good books?"

"You can read?"

"Of course I can."

"Right. Well, my sister has two young kids. Maybe I could see if they have anything suitable?"

"No, no. Not children's books. I was thinking more along the lines of Tolstoy, or maybe Dickens, or some Shakespeare—"

"You read that kind of book?"

"Of course. Don't you?"

"Err — yes, of course. All the time."

"So—if you could see your way clear to getting me a few books, that would be great."

"Won't you have a problem with the size of the books? Will I even be able to get them into your cage?"

"You'll need to get the rodent edition."

"Is that a thing?"

"Of course. I suppose I could have audio books, but they can be rather expensive. No, the rodent edition will be fine."

"Okay then. I'll see what I can do. Bye then, Hamlet."

"Bye, Jill."

I made my way outside, and stopped to gather my thoughts. I was now book shopping for a hamster. My crazy had just gone up a couple more notches.

***

Grandma burst into my office. She was not a happy camper.

"Have you seen this?" she said, throwing a newspaper down on my desk.

"What is it?"

"Read it for yourself."

It was today's edition of The Candle.

"Look at those headlines!" She prodded the offending article with her crooked finger. "Read it! Just read it!"

The headline read, *'Town Hall Candidate Gone Rogue?'* I skip-read the article, which all but accused Grandma of the misuse of magic in the human world. All of Grandma's new innovations were very suspicious, and for a long time, I'd suspected magic was involved. But how had The Candle got hold of the story? Who had told them?

"So?" She spat out the word. "What do you think?"

"I—err—I don't know. What do you want to do about it?"

"We're going to deny it, of course, but that's not the point. Where do you think they got that story from?"

"I don't have a clue."

"That's the problem. You're completely clueless. I'll tell you where the story came from. It came from your friend Dexter Long."

"But we had an agreement that there would be no dirty tricks, no smear campaign."

"Jill, you have an awful lot to learn. You can't trust the word of a campaign manager. It's their job to lie, cheat, and do anything it takes to get their candidate elected. Which is precisely what you should have been doing, instead of being all 'Miss Goody Two Shoes' about it."

"I still can't believe he did it."

"Why don't you go around there, and find out for yourself? See what he has to say about it."

"I will. I'll do that. I'm sure he wasn't behind it."

***

"Yes, it's rather good, isn't it?" Dexter Long laughed. "I thought you'd like it."

"You mean you did feed this to The Candle?"

"Of course I did! It's the killer blow. Your candidate may as well throw in the towel right now. Lance Boyle is all but elected."

"But we had an agreement."

"Oh dearie me." He laughed. "As a campaign manager, I have to say you make a good P.I."

"But you promised there'd be no dirty tricks."

"Yeah well. What are you going to do about it?"

I wanted to slap the smile off his face, but he'd no doubt have a photographer close at hand, and then the next edition of the Candle would have a photo of me assaulting him, on the front page. I could see the headline now: *Mirabel Millbright's campaign manager is a thug.*

I'd been completely outmanoeuvred and outwitted. So much for my faith in human nature.

***

The arts and crafts show was in the local community hall. Kathy had taken Lizzie to the competitors' area to submit her entry for the under tens competition. Meanwhile, I'd been left in charge of Mikey who, as always, was playing his drum. He'd played it in the car all the way there, and he'd been playing it ever since we'd arrived.

"Mikey!" I yelled.

"Pardon? Did you say something, Auntie Jill?"

"Yes. Do you think you could stop playing that drum for a minute?"

"Sorry, I can't hear you."

How did Kathy put up with this? A little magic was called for.

"Oh, no!" he cried out.

"What's the matter, Mikey?" I enquired—all innocent-like.

"There's something wrong with my drum! It's gone all

spongy."

"What do you mean, spongy?"

"Look." He pressed the top of the drum which now had the texture of a sponge.

"I think you've worn it out, Mikey. You must have played it so much it's gone all soft."

"But I love my drum."

Oh no. It looked like he was about to cry. Kathy would kill me.

"It's okay. I know someone who can mend it."

"Do you really, Auntie Jill?"

"Yes. If you let me have it, I'll take to him."

"Can I go with you?"

"No, you have to stay here. I'll only be a minute. I'll take it to the drum repair man, and then we'll be able to pick it up on our way out."

"Okay. Are you sure he'll be able to mend it?"

"Yeah, I'm positive."

Mikey passed me the drum, and I told him to stay put. Then, I rushed outside and put it in the boot of my car. Fortunately, I made it back before Kathy and Lizzie returned.

"Did he say he could mend it, Auntie Jill?" Mikey had a worried look on his face, and I felt a pang of guilt. Who was I kidding? I felt no guilt whatsoever—I was just relieved to be shut of that stupid drum.

"Yes. He said it would be ready by the time we go home."

Moments later, Kathy and Lizzie were back. Lizzie was all smiles.

"The lady said my kangadillo was fantastic!"

"Was she wearing very thick glasses?" I said.

"Jill!" Kathy gave me a look.

"I didn't mean anything. I just wondered—"

"I know what you meant," Kathy said. "I think Lizzie is in with a good chance of winning a prize." She stared at Mikey, trying to work out what was different about him. "Where's your drum, Mikey?"

"Auntie Jill has taken it to the drum repair man."

Kathy glared at me. 'Drum repair man?' she mouthed.

I nodded.

"Look kids!" She pointed. "They have refreshments over there. Why don't you go and get something?" As soon as they were out of earshot, she turned to me. "What have you done with his drum, Jill?"

"Nothing. It's in the car. Mikey said he was bored with it."

"He just said you'd taken it to the *drum repair man*?"

"You must have misheard him. I'm sure he said that I'd 'put it in the van'. He probably thinks my car is a van."

Fortunately, before Kathy could interrogate me any further, the kids came back.

"There you are, Auntie Jill. I got you a cake." Lizzie held out what looked like a rectangular piece of rubber, with a little bit of icing on top.

"That looks delicious," I said, looking around for a bin.

The next two hours felt like an eternity, as Kathy and the kids dragged me from one stand to the next. The tables held an assortment of soft toys, jewellery, and various knitted and crocheted items; none of which I would have given house room. But I was under strict instructions from Kathy to be complimentary about everything on display.

"How much more of this is there?" I said.

"What's wrong with you, Jill? The people here have spent days creating all of these lovely things."

"But it's all rubbish."

"Shh! Don't let anyone hear you say that."

"But it's true!"

"It might be, but you don't want to hurt people's feelings, do you?"

If I had to suffer, why shouldn't they?

"Ladies and gentlemen." Came a voice from the front of the hall. "It's time to announce this year's prize winners."

He spent the next twenty minutes giving out prizes for all manner of categories: best tea cosy, best tapestry, best snood—. The list was endless.

"And finally, we come to the children's category. This year the prize for the ten and under age group goes to Lizzie Brooks for the kangadillo. The judges all thought this was a very exciting and imaginative piece of work."

"Well done, Lizzie," Kathy said. "Go and collect your prize."

Lizzie trotted off to the stage, took the small silver cup and held it above her head. Kathy cheered. She looked at me, so I cheered too.

"See," Kathy said. "I told you it was artistic."

The world had gone bonkers.

Chapter 15

What was with the roads this morning? I'd been sitting in a queue of traffic, which was barely moving, for the last fifteen minutes. Everything seemed to have ground to a halt. People in cars all around me were pressing their horns. As if *that* was going to do any good. Eventually, I pulled into a side street, and parked. I was going to walk the rest of the way.

As I got closer to my office, the traffic was still gridlocked. I'd never seen anything like it. Eventually, I spotted a harassed-looking policeman.

"What's the problem? What's causing all the delays?"

"Don't ask," he said.

"I just did."

"Scarves."

Huh?

"I did warn you not to ask."

"What do you mean, *scarves*?"

"There's some kind of charity event going on involving scarves: 'Scarves Around Washbridge' or something like that. I'd never even heard of it until this morning." He gave a deep sigh. "I wish I still hadn't. Look, I'm sorry, but I'm very busy." With that he walked away.

Mrs V had mentioned Scarves Around Washbridge a while ago, but what exactly was it? And why would it cause hold-ups like this? Seconds later, I had my answer. A number of people were desperately trying to remove a huge scarf which was spanning the high street, blocking traffic in both directions. One man was attacking it with a saw. Several other people were also trying to cut it, but none of them was having any success. It was as though it had been knitted in some sort of indestructible yarn.

When I eventually got into the office, Mrs V was looking out of the window.

"I got stuck in traffic," I said.

She turned to face me. "Oh, Jill. It's terrible! Look what's happening out there. And everyone's blaming me. I've already had a dozen phone calls. People think it's my fault. I'm not the organiser; I just agreed to open the event."

"There's a giant scarf blocking the road. I don't know what it's made from, but no one can cut through it."

"I know. They're all asking what I intend to do about it. What *can* I do? I didn't even know it was there until I received the first phone call. The whole idea behind Scarves Around Washbridge is that people should wrap them around lamp posts, post boxes, telephone boxes, and even buildings. They're not supposed to put them across the road. Who would do something like that?"

"Do you really need to ask?"

"Your grandmother? I've tried to contact her, but she's not answering her phone. It wouldn't surprise me if she'd done this deliberately, just because they didn't ask her to open the event."

That sounded about right. In fact, it was just the kind of thing she would do.

"Don't fret about it, Mrs V. It isn't your fault. I'll go to 'Ever' now and see if I can find her."

"Who trod on your bunions?" Kathy said when I charged, red-faced through the door of Ever A Wool Moment.

"Don't mention bunions to me."

They conjured up bad memories of Christmas. What do you mean you didn't read the Christmas book? You'd better not let Winky find out.

"Where is she?"

"By *she*, I'm guessing you mean your dearest grandmother?"

"Who else?"

"She's in the back—still on the campaign trail."

"Right!" I started towards the door.

"She said she wasn't to be disturbed."

"Tough!"

"Well, if it isn't my campaign manager." Grandma had her bare feet resting on the desk. "You've come just in time to apply my ointment."

"You can forget that."

"To *what* do we owe the pleasure of your company, then?"

"You know full well. Have you seen the traffic jams out there?"

"I've been too busy with the election to look outside. So should you be."

"That stupid scarf of yours is blocking the main road."

"Generating a lot of publicity for 'Scarves around Washbridge' though, I'll wager."

"Poor old Mrs V is getting it in the neck from everyone. They all think it's her fault."

"Well, she *is* the face of the campaign, after all."

"You have to remove that scarf, and you have to do it right now."

Her gaze fixed mine, and I feared the worst.

"Or what?"

"Or—err—or—I won't be your campaign manager."

"You've already agreed to do it."

"Well, I'll just un-agree."

Her face flushed red, and her wart began to throb. Never a good sign.

"I mean it!" I said, trying to hide my nerves.

Grandma took a deep breath, and then smiled—the scariest smile you ever did see.

"The scarf has served its purpose. It will be front page news tomorrow. Maybe now the committee will see sense, and appoint me next year."

"So you'll remove it?"

"It's already gone."

"All sorted, Mrs V," I said when I got back to the office. "The traffic seems to be moving again now."

"Thank you, Jill. I take it that it *was* your grandmother's doing?"

"Yes, but she hadn't realised the pandemonium it would cause. She's very sorry."

Mrs V gave me a look. "I very much doubt that, dear."

***

You'd think by now that I'd be used to my crazy cat, but just when I thought things couldn't get any more insane, Winky managed to take it to another level.

"What are you doing?"

"Shush! I'm busy."

"What's with all of those mirrors?"

He was surrounded by four of them, and was shuffling around, straining his neck, obviously trying to see something.

"Is there a problem?"

"Of course there's a problem. Can't you see it?"

"Not really, no."

"Just look at me! It's obvious."

I was clearly missing something. He looked his usual one-eyed, crazy self to me. I couldn't see anything different about him.

I shrugged.

"I'm losing my fur!"

"Where?"

"Around the back there. There's a bald spot. You must be able to see it?"

I looked a little closer, and eventually spotted a tiny area where the fur was missing. It was miniscule, and barely noticeable.

"It's nothing."

"Nothing? What do you mean it's nothing? How can I let anyone see me looking like this? What will Bella think?"

"I'd be amazed if she even noticed it."

"It's no good talking to you. You're just a human."

"Hey! Who are you calling a human?"

"Sup, human—all the same to me. Why should I expect you to notice when you came out with your hair looking like that?"

"What's wrong with my hair?"

"The very fact that you have to ask just proves my point."

I let the remark go. "So, what do you intend to do about your little problem, then?"

"I've been looking online for a cure for feline baldness."

"*Baldness* is a bit of an exaggeration."

"What would you call it?"

"A small gap in your fur?"

"A gap? I can't let anyone see me with a 'gap' in my fur."

"But you hardly ever go out."

"People can still see me on Skype."

"You've got Skype?"

"Of course I've got Skype! It's on your computer."

"I know it's on *my* computer, but since when did you have a Skype account on *my* computer?"

"I don't have time to get into that right now. I need to find a cure for this baldness."

"Have you tried *BaldFelines.com*?"

"I suppose you think that's funny."

I did actually. "No, it's obviously not a laughing matter." I laughed.

"I might have known I'd get no sympathy from you."

***

Mrs V popped her head around the door. "Lady Phoebe is here to see you."

"Oh right, would you ask her to come through, please."

I'd asked Lady Phoebe to come to my office, but not to mention it to her husband. She'd been a little surprised and hesitant at first, but in the end she'd agreed. I thought it was only fair to do it this way—after all, I didn't want to embarrass her. If I could have a word in private, then maybe we could resolve things without any unpleasantness.

"Good morning, young lady," Lady Phoebe said. "This

is all very cloak and dagger. I was rather surprised when you asked to see me without Cuthbert."

"I'm sure you'll understand when I tell you what I've discovered. Please take a seat."

"Thank you. What is that thing?"

"That's Winky, my cat."

"He's rather ugly, isn't he?"

"Who does she think she is?" Winky said.

I shushed him.

"Sorry?" Lady Phoebe said.

"Nothing, I just sneezed."

"So what is it that you have to tell me, young lady?"

"It's rather delicate and a little bit embarrassing."

"No need for you to be embarrassed, dear. I've seen it all and done most of it. Just spit it out. What's bothering you?"

"Actually, I thought it might be embarrassing for you."

"For me? What do you mean?"

"It's about the missing vase."

"Have you found it?"

"No, but I suspect I know who may have taken it."

"Really? Who?"

"Well, actually." I hesitated. "I think you did."

"I beg your pardon?" She looked aghast.

"I think *you* took it."

"Would you care to explain yourself?"

"I spoke to Lady Bunty. She and her husband told me they stopped off in Winminster on their way back from Ladies' Day at Ascot. They said they saw you coming out of the antique shop."

"They saw me?" she said.

"Yes. Climbing into a green Porsche."

"What exactly are you suggesting?"

"Your gardener, Roger Tyler has a green Porsche."

"Let me get this straight. You think that I'm having some kind of a 'fling' with Roger Tyler? And that I stole my own antiques and sold them to finance this *affair*?"

"That would explain how your gardener could afford a car like that."

"Hmm, and I assume you didn't want Sir Cuthbert to join us today because you thought it might be embarrassing for me if he found out about this?"

"Precisely."

"Interesting theory. Would you just give me a moment?" she said.

I was beginning to have serious doubts—I'd expected her to break down and confess. Instead, she reached into her handbag and took out a phone.

"Cuthbert, it's me. You'll never guess where I am. No, no, not there. I'm with that private investigator of yours. The crazy woman thinks that *I* stole the vase. And, there's more. Apparently, I'm also having an affair with the gardener. Yes, dear, that's what I thought. Look, I'm going to pass this phone to her now. Would you mind telling the *private investigator* where you and I were on Ladies' Day at Ascot this year? Okay, passing you over now."

By now all the colour had drained from my face. I knew I'd got this badly wrong, but I had no idea why.

"Hello," I said, wishing the ground would open up and swallow me.

"What on earth are you doing Jill?" Sir Cuthbert shouted. "Why would you accuse Phoebe of stealing her own vase? Dear me, I shall have to speak to the colonel. He told me that you were top notch. Anyway, as for

Ladies' Day, Phoebe and I were in Edinburgh. All day, and the next day too. Although, I'm not sure what difference that makes."

"Oh, I see. Thank you."

I handed the phone back to Lady Phoebe.

"I think we're done here, young lady." She stood up.

"I'm sorry, Lady Phoebe. I may have got this wrong."

"You *may* have got this wrong? You *may* have?"

"I obviously *have* got this wrong. I'm deeply sorry."

"I assume you won't be sending us a bill?"

"No, of course not."

"Right. Goodbye then."

With that, she stormed out of the office.

How had I got it so wrong? I'd been sure that she'd been stealing her own antiques to finance her affair with Roger Tyler.

"Another satisfied customer," Winky said.

"Shut up, baldy."

Chapter 16

An hour later, and I was still reeling from my meeting with Lady Phoebe.

"I really messed up, Winky."

"Do I look like I care? I have more important things to worry about. Just look at this fur!"

"I thought you were going to buy a tonic?"

"I'm still searching for one, but I haven't found anything yet."

"You'll have to get off my computer. I have some would-be clients arriving any moment."

"Let's hope they didn't bump into that old gal on their way here. I doubt she'd give you a glowing reference."

"Don't rub it in. I feel bad enough already. Anyway, you'll have to get off there before they arrive."

"Are you trying to tell me that your *would-be clients* are more important than my fur loss?"

"Without a shadow of a doubt." I gently nudged him off the desk.

"Hey! I could report you."

"As soon as I've finished with my clients, you can carry on your search."

"Why don't you ask them?"

"Ask who?"

"The people who are coming to see you."

"Ask them what?"

"If they know of any good products for curing fur loss."

"Yeah, because that's likely."

"Just ask them."

"I'm trying to win a new client here. What sort of impression would it make if the first thing I do when they walk through the door is ask them if they know of a cure for feline fur loss?"

"If you care for me at all, you'll ask them."

Before I could respond, the door opened, and Mrs V showed the couple in. The woman was small and mouse-like. The man was a good nine inches taller, and completely bald. I glanced at Winky who shook his head in despair.

"Mr and Mrs Coot?" I said.

"Scoot, actually," the man said.

"Oh, sorry. My receptionist's handwriting can be a challenge at times."

"I'm Walter and this is Elizabeth."

The woman managed a weak smile, but didn't speak.

"Please have a seat. How can I help?"

"We're going to lose our house," the woman said. She was close to tears.

"It's okay, Liz." The man put his hand on hers. "We've lived in Palm Close for the last ten years, and we've been really happy there. But unless you can help us, we'll probably have to move out."

"I don't want to move." The woman began to sob.

"It's all right, Liz. We're going to get this sorted."

"What exactly is the problem? Is it a financial issue?"

"No, nothing like that. There are twelve houses on the street, and most of the other residents have been there as long as we have. We love living there. Or, at least, we *used to*."

"What happened?"

"I'm not sure." He hesitated. "You'll think I'm crazy."

If only this man knew how insane my whole life was, he'd realise it would have to be something truly spectacular for me to find whatever he had to tell me crazy.

"Go on. Try me."

"It started about three months ago. The couple who live directly across from us, who we'd known for years, suddenly upped and left. Then the same thing happened with our next door neighbours. We'd been friends with Jessie and Michael for years, and they'd always said they'd never move. But they too decided to leave. The same thing has happened at two more houses. There's hardly anyone left."

"It's rather a coincidence, I grant you, but stranger things have happened. Has anyone moved into the vacated properties?"

"No, they're all still empty."

"I'm still not sure why you feel you have to move out."

"It's haunted!" Mrs Scoot blurted out.

"Haunted? Have you actually seen a ghost?"

"No," her husband said. "We haven't seen anything. Not really. I've never believed in ghosts. I've always thought it was nonsense. But there are things happening in that house which I just can't explain. It's making Liz ill; I don't think we can take much more. And, now we've had an offer from someone wanting to buy the house. I don't want to sell, but I don't see how we can stay there."

"Who did the offer come from?"

"I don't actually know. It came via a firm of solicitors, who wouldn't name their client. It isn't a bad offer. It's roughly the market value, maybe a little under, but we don't want to leave our home. That's why we've come to see you. I don't really know what I expect you to do, but we have to try to do something. Do you think you can help, or do you think we're crazy?"

"Not at all. No one would blame you for not wanting to leave the house you love."

"So, will you take the case?"

"Of course."

After they'd gone, Winky jumped back on the desk, and began searching for potions online. Meanwhile, I mulled over what Mr and Mrs Scoot had told me. Little did they know that I had every reason to believe in ghosts, but there was something about the whole story which didn't ring true.

***

I got a phone call from Pearl.

"Jill! It's Jethro time. Hurry!"

How pathetic! Why get so excited just because Aunt Lucy's gardener was working at her house today. He was only a man after all.

"Yeah, come on," Amber shouted. "Or you're going to miss him."

As if I would stoop so low.

"I'm rather busy, girls. I don't know if I can make it."

"Your loss," Pearl said, and she ended the call.

Silly girls. It was about time they grew up. I tried to focus on the papers in front of me, but it was no good.

"I've just remembered something I have to do," I said to Winky on my way to the door.

He rolled his eye. "Are you off to ogle that gardener again?"

"No, of course not. I just remembered I have an—err—

appointment at the—err—optician."

Winky smirked; he wasn't buying that for one minute.

I lost no time in magicking myself over to Aunt Lucy's. I was in such a hurry that I actually stumbled into the twins when I arrived.

"Well, well, well, look who's here," Pearl said.

"I thought you weren't interested." Amber giggled.

"I'm not. It's just that I had something else to do in Candlefield."

"Of course you did," Amber said.

"Where is he, anyway?"

"I just saw him heading towards the back gate. Quick."

Aunt Lucy was already at the window. What would Lester think if he saw her ogling the gardener?

"Hello, Jill," she said, without once taking her eyes off the window.

"Admiring the flower beds?"

She either didn't hear me or chose to ignore the jibe.

We spent the next few minutes jostling one another to get the best view.

"He has someone with him," Pearl said.

"Where?"

"Look! There behind him. Did you know about this, Mum?" Amber said.

"Actually, now you mention it, I do remember Jethro saying that he'd taken on an apprentice, but I didn't realise he'd be helping him with my garden."

"What's he like?" Pearl said. "Is he hot too?"

"I can't get a good look at him." Amber was straining her neck, trying to get a better view. "He's a lot shorter than Jethro; much smaller build too. And that baseball cap doesn't really do anything for him."

"Worth a closer look though," Pearl said.

"You two are terrible." I interrupted their evaluation of the newcomer. "If William and Alan could see you now, they'd disown you."

"You can talk!" Amber said, "What about Jack, Drake and whoever else you have in tow this week?"

"I don't have anyone 'in tow'. And like I said, I didn't come here to see Jethro, I just—"

"Don't give us that. We can see straight through your fairy stories," Amber said. "Anyway, if William and I ever do split up, I might let Jethro take me out."

Pearl giggled. "You'd *let* him? What makes you think he'd want to take *you* out?"

"Why wouldn't he?"

"Just look at him! He could have his pick of any woman in Candlefield. He's never going to pick you."

"It's possible."

"In your dreams! You might get a date with his apprentice, if you're lucky."

"Look!" Aunt Lucy pointed.

The apprentice had taken off his baseball cap, and put it on the fence. As he did, his long hair cascaded down over his shoulders, and it became immediately apparent that *he* was actually a *she*. She was petite, and very pretty.

"It's a girl!" Amber said.

"What's Jethro doing with a girl?" Pearl huffed. "He can't work with a girl!"

"I'm pretty sure he can work with whoever he wants." I laughed.

"It's not right. How can we have 'Jethro time' if he's got a girl with him?"

"She's very pretty," Aunt Lucy said.

"Not that pretty." Pearl screwed up her nose. "Look, there's a spot on her chin."

"Yes, and her hair is greasy," Amber said.

"So, you two aren't jealous then?" I grinned.

"Of course not! She obviously only *works* with him. I doubt he even notices she's a girl."

"Oh, I think he's noticed," I said. "Look at the way he's looking at her."

***

Once we'd realised that Jethro's apprentice was a girl, we felt a little awkward staring at them. One by one, we all moved away and took a seat in the kitchen.

"I think it's disgusting," Amber said.

"What is?" Aunt Lucy was pouring the tea.

"Jethro bringing a girl with him. What was he thinking?"

"She's here to learn."

"She should find something more suitable."

"Really, Pearl!" I was flabbergasted. "I can't believe you just said that! That's very sexist."

"I didn't mean it like that. I meant there are plenty of other jobs she could do which don't require her to work alongside *our* Jethro."

Aunt Lucy rolled her eyes at her daughter, and then turned to me. "Jill, I wanted to ask you a favour."

"What's that?"

"Lester and I were thinking of having a weekend away."

"How come you didn't tell us?" Amber said.

"I'm sure you two don't tell me *everything* you and your fiancés do."

The twins blushed.

"Anyway, as I was saying, Jill. I wondered if you would look after the house while we're away?"

"What?" Amber almost choked on her drink.

"What do you mean, if *she*'ll look after the house?" Pearl said. "Why can't *we* look after it? We're your daughters."

Aunt Lucy took a deep breath. "Don't you remember what happened the last time I asked you two to look after the house?"

"It was only a small party," Amber said.

"Yeah," Pearl said. "There can't have been more than half a dozen people."

"There were thirty-seven."

"*We* didn't invite them all."

"That's irrelevant. There were thirty-seven people in the house when I came back early."

"Yes, but if we'd known you were going to come back early—"

"You were supposed to be looking after the house. You both promised that you wouldn't have friends around here."

"But—"

"But nothing. You two have had your chance, and proven you can't be trusted."

"Well, at least we know where we stand," Pearl said. "We might as well go now then. We know when we're not wanted, don't we, Amber?"

"We sure do!"

The two of them stood up, and stormed out, slamming the door behind them.

"Oh dear. I think I may have upset them." Aunt Lucy laughed. She didn't appear to be too concerned.

"Are you sure you want me to do this?" I said.

"Yes. I trust you, Jill. I know that if you promise to do something, you will. And, I know you're not the kind of person to throw wild parties."

What did she mean, *'not the kind of person to throw wild parties'*? I had a horrible feeling that translated as: being boring and past it.

"So, are you sure you're okay with this, Jill?"

"Yes, of course I'll do it."

"Great. That's settled then."

"What about the twins?"

"Never mind those two. They'll get over it. They always do."

Chapter 17

I wasn't sure what kind of a reception I'd get when I got back to Cuppy C, but I feared the worst. Amber and Pearl were sitting at a window table chatting away, until they spotted me.

"Hi, you two."

"Traitor!" Pearl said.

"It's not my fault that Aunt Lucy asked me to look after the house."

They both glared at me, but then giggled.

"It's okay. We don't blame you," Amber said. "We blame Mum. Why doesn't she trust us?"

"It's just a wild guess, but maybe it has something to do with what happened last time? When you had a party?"

"It wasn't *really* a party. It was just a gathering of friends," Amber said.

"These friends—were any of them drunk?"

"Some of them, possibly."

"And did anything get damaged?"

"Well—there was that vase. And the mirror. Oh, and the carpet, and the back door. Nothing much really."

I laughed. "It's really hard to understand why she was upset."

"Anyway, we don't care, do we, Pearl?" Amber said.

"No. We've got better things to do. *We* have fiancés *and* a social life."

"I have a social life."

"Really?" They looked at each other and giggled again.

"Anyway, I'd better go and see to Barry."

Barry didn't come running to greet me like he usually

did. I found him lying next to the bed, with his head on his front paws, looking very sorry for himself.

"Barry?"

"Humph."

"What's wrong?"

"Nothing."

"Come on, Barry. This isn't like you. Something must be wrong."

"If you must know, it's Hamlet."

"Has something happened to him? Is he okay?"

"He's fine."

"So what's wrong?"

"He doesn't like to play or talk to me. He ignores me most of the time."

"I'm sure that's not true."

"It is. He's started a book club, and he won't let me join."

"A what?"

"A book club. I don't like books—they're boring. I like to go for walks—to the park. And, I like eating. I'm not really bothered about books."

"Where is he now?"

"The twins have moved him into the box room. He said I was making so much noise that he couldn't concentrate on his reading."

"Okay, you stay here while I go and have a chat with the hamster. I'm sure we can sort this out."

The box room wasn't really big enough to be a bedroom, so it was used for storage. I found the hamster's cage on a shelf; he had company.

"Hammy."

He sighed.

"Sorry. I mean, Hamlet."

"Hello, Jill. What brings you here?"

"I've just been talking to Barry."

"Really? That must have been a riveting conversation."

"Who are all of your friends?"

There were five other hamsters sitting in a circle. Each of them was holding a book—rodent edition, obviously.

"Just a few like-minded hamsters. We meet a couple of times a week. I suppose you could call it a book club. We like to discuss the merits of various novels. Today we're discussing War and Peace. Are you familiar with it, Jill?"

"Me? Err—well—it's been a while since I—err—no."

He looked disappointed; I was beginning to understand how Barry felt.

"Anyway, was there something else you wanted?"

"No, not really."

"Right. Well, shut the door on your way out, would you?"

"Sure. Okay. Bye, Hamlet."

**

I was doing my best to forget about the mess I'd made of the missing vase case. To cheer myself up, I'd helped myself to the largest blueberry muffin that Cuppy C had to offer, but it wasn't helping. Maybe I was in the wrong career. Maybe I wasn't cut out to be a P.I. after all. How could I have made such a stupid mistake? What would my father have thought? He would never have jumped in feet first like that. What made it worse was that I'd let the colonel down. He'd recommended me to Sir Cuthbert. What would he have to say when I saw him next?

"Are you okay, Jill?" It was Daze. She was by herself today.

"Hi, Daze. Yeah, I'm okay."

"You don't look it. Mind if I join you?"

"Sure. Have a seat." Daze got herself a coffee, but resisted the muffins. Her willpower was obviously much stronger than mine.

"What's wrong?" she pressed.

"I don't really want to talk about it. Just a case gone bad, I messed up big time. Anyway, enough about me. How are things with you? When I saw you at the Punch and Judy show, you mentioned that you were after a rogue witch. What did you call her? Mona?"

"Mona Lisa? Oh, yeah. We caught her."

"Is that her real name?"

"No, of course not. I don't actually remember what her real name is. She's always been known as Mona Lisa because she has a particular skill set. She's able to replicate works of art, so that they're indistinguishable from the real thing. She plies her trade in the human world, and usually stays under the radar."

A little bell was ringing in the back of my head. "So what does she forge?"

"Anything really, but she specialises in statues, vases — that kind of thing."

Suddenly, everything was starting to click into place.

"I don't suppose you have a photo of her, do you?"

"Yeah. I have a few on my phone. I can email you one when we're back in Washbridge. Why do you want it?"

"Just a hunch I'd like to check out."

"I could email you a photo, but I should warn you, she makes your grandma look pretty."

***

The green Porsche was parked outside Roger Tyler's house. I had to get this right, if I messed up again, my career as a P.I. would be over for good. Before I got out of my car, I checked the photo which Daze had emailed to me, then I cast the 'doppelganger' spell. Daze had been right; Mona was criminally ugly.

"Where have you been?" Tyler said, when he answered the door to me.

Exactly the reaction I'd hoped for; now I knew my hunch was right.

"I got called away."

"What do you mean called away? I've had a private investigator around here asking questions about the vase. Come inside quick before someone sees you."

I followed him into the flat.

"Where were you?" he said. "Why didn't you contact me?"

"I had to leave suddenly. It was a matter of life and death."

"*I'd* have been dead if they'd caught me with the vase."

"You should have taken it back!"

"I would have done, but that dozy butler got up early, and saw it was missing."

"What do we do now?" I said.

"Once I've got the duplicate, I'll leave it somewhere, and give Sir Cuthbert an anonymous tip-off. Once he *thinks* he has the vase back, he'll tell the police to drop the case."

"I'd better get cracking with the copy then. Where's the

original? Is it still here?"

"Of course it isn't! As soon as it was reported missing, I had to move it pronto."

"Where is it then? I want to get this over with."

"Don't you think I do?" He took out a scrap of paper, grabbed a pen, and scribbled an address down. "Be there at seven o'clock tonight. Don't be late, and make sure no one follows you."

With that, he practically pushed me out of the door.

Once I was back in my car, I made a call to Jack Maxwell. Mr Tyler had a big surprise coming to him.

***

I could tell something was wrong when I arrived at the office.

"What's wrong, Mrs V?"

"Look at these," she said. "This is just a small fraction of them. I've had dozens of letters from irate motorists who were late getting to work on Scarves Around Washbridge day. They say it was my fault that they were late, and they're threatening to sue me. And it's all because of that stupid scarf your grandmother tied across the road."

"You mustn't let it get to you. It wasn't your fault."

"These people don't know that. They see me as the face of the event, and assume I was responsible. I'm going to tell the organising committee that I won't do it again next year."

"You mustn't do that. You can't let Grandma win; that's just what she wants. She only did it so you'd quit, and she'd be able to open the event next year."

"I don't care. This has spoiled it for me. I used to look

forward to Scarves Around Washbridge. It was fun to see all the scarves wrapped around lamp posts and telegraph poles. But now, the only thing people will remember is the traffic chaos it caused."

"What do you intend to do with the letters?"

"I shall reply to each one individually, and apologise."

"You really don't need to go to all that trouble."

"It's the least I can do, Jill."

"Okay. Well, I'm really sorry it happened."

"It wasn't your fault. We both know who was responsible."

What's wrong with misery guts out there," Winky said, in his usual compassionate manner.

"Mrs V is upset because she's being blamed for something that wasn't her fault."

"Oh, cry me a river. She should be grateful she doesn't have something really serious to worry about — like I do."

"What do you have to worry about apart from whether or not I remember your full cream milk?"

"Have you forgotten my fur situation already?"

"As if I could forget something *so* important."

"I'm not sure you appreciate the gravity of the situation."

"Trust me, I do."

"Well then, you'll be pleased to hear that I've found a potion which is guaranteed to restore fur."

"I'm absolutely delighted. I've been losing sleep over it."

"It was quite expensive, but it's okay — I used your credit card."

"You did what?"

"I knew you wouldn't mind under the circumstances."

"My credit card is already maxed out. Where am I meant to find the money to pay it off?"

"Here's an idea. Why don't you find some clients?"

"I'll have you know I'm working on a case right now."

"Well, chop-chop. You'd better get started. You have fur restorer to pay for."

Chapter 18

The Scoots had given me the name and phone number of the couple who used to live across the road from them: a Mr and Mrs Nutt. I rang the number and spoke to Phillip Nutt, but he said that there was nothing to tell. They'd decided it was time for a change, so had sold up and moved on. Something in his voice told me there was more to it than that, but even though I pressed him, he wouldn't say any more, and he refused to meet with me.

I tried again a couple more times, using burner phones so he wouldn't recognise the number. The next day, on the third attempt, I got lucky. It was Patricia Nutt who answered the phone this time.

"Hi, my name's Jill Gooder. I'm a private investigator."

"Didn't you ring my husband yesterday?"

"Yes I did."

"He isn't here at the moment, but he'll be back shortly. He said you wanted to talk about Palm Close."

"That's right. The Scoots came to see me."

"Walter and Liz? They were great neighbours. We were sorry to leave them behind."

"I don't know if you've spoken to them recently, but they've been having a spot of bother."

"What kind of bother?"

"Before I get into that, can I ask why you decided to leave Palm Close?"

There was silence for the longest moment. When she did eventually speak, she fed me the exact same lines as her husband had earlier: it was time for a change, it was time to move on.

"Mrs Nutt, I'm sorry to press you, but I think there's

more to it than that. And I believe that whatever it is you're holding back may be connected to the problems that the Scoots are now experiencing."

She hesitated. "Phillip doesn't like me to talk about it. He wouldn't be happy if he found out that I'd spoken to you."

"Would it be possible for us to meet somewhere? Just for a few minutes."

"I suppose so, but my husband must never know."

"I understand. Where would be a good place?"

"Somewhere in the city centre. My husband works on the outskirts of Washbridge, so it's unlikely he'd see us there."

"What about a coffee shop? Are you a fan of percussion?"

"Percussion?"

"Never mind." On reflection, I decided the instruments might be too much of a distraction—probably better to meet her somewhere a little quieter. "There's a small coffee shop close to my office—maybe we could meet there?"

"Yes, okay. When?"

"Could you make it this afternoon at say three o'clock?"

"Yes, I guess so."

I gave her the name of the coffee shop, and we agreed to meet later that day.

***

That afternoon, I arrived at the coffee shop ten minutes early; Patricia Nutt was already there. She'd found a corner seat as far away from the window as possible.

"Patricia?" I said.

She nodded.

"Would you like another drink?"

"No, I'm fine." She forced a smile. "Thanks."

I got myself a coffee and joined her. "Thanks for seeing me."

"That's okay. I'd like to help the Scoots if I can."

"Where are you living now?"

"In an apartment in the Westside development. It's very nice, but not a patch on Palm Close. I loved that house. I had thought we'd live there for the rest of our lives." She took a sip of tea. "What kind of problems are the Scoots having?"

"They think their house is haunted."

I thought she might be shocked or even burst out laughing. Instead, I got the distinct impression that she wasn't surprised in the least.

"The exact same thing happened to us. If someone had told me a year ago that this could happen, I'd have laughed in their face."

"Did you actually see any ghosts?"

"We both saw something. Something very scary. We simply couldn't stay there any longer. We had to get out."

"What about the house? It can't have been easy to sell it."

"It was surprisingly easy. We'd no sooner made the decision to leave than we were approached by a solicitor, acting on behalf of an anonymous buyer."

"Did you ever find out who that was?"

"No, we still have no idea, but they gave us a fair price, so we sold. As far as I know, the house is still empty."

This was a familiar story. Something definitely wasn't

right.

"Will you be able to help the Scoots?" she said.

"I don't know, but I'll do my best."

"I hope for their sakes you can. I'd hate to think they'll be driven out like we were."

I thanked her for her help, and promised not to let her husband know we'd spoken.

***

"Remind me again why we're doing this," Pearl said.

"You know why." I was sick of hearing the twins moaning. "It's to help Grandma."

"But *why* are we helping Grandma?" Amber said.

"Girls." I sighed. "We had this same conversation last night, and again this morning. She's standing for election to the Town Council, and she's asked us to help."

"When does she ever help us?" Pearl said.

"You two have short memories. Don't you remember when Best Cakes opened, and you asked her for marketing advice?"

"You mean when she made us dress up as cupcakes?"

"Yes. But it worked, didn't it?"

"I suppose so." Amber huffed.

"You really are ungrateful. Look, it won't take long. All we have to do is hand out these leaflets."

"But it's freezing out here."

"Stop moaning. The sooner we finish the sooner we can go back inside."

"That's easier said than done." Pearl sighed. "Nobody wants one. And can you blame them?"

It was true. Nobody did. It didn't help that Grandma's face was plastered across the front. The universal reaction so far had been: 'Ugh, no thank you'.

"Look, I tell you what," I said. "We should split up."

We were standing in the market square; we'd been there for about half an hour.

"Pearl, you take that side of the square. Amber, you take the other side. I'll stay here. Hand out your leaflets, and when they're all gone, we can meet back here."

"How come," Amber said. "You get to stay here?"

"Yeah, could it have anything to do with the cake shop right behind you?"

"What cake shop?" I tried to sound surprised. "I didn't realise there was one."

"So, you didn't realise that the blueberry muffins you've been staring at for the last fifteen minutes were in a cake shop? What did you think it was, a pet shop?"

"I hadn't noticed any blueberry muffins." I lied.

They both laughed.

"Of course you hadn't," Amber said. "Just so you know, I've counted them, and when I get back, if there are any missing, we'll know you've had one."

The girls marched off in opposite directions. I waited until they were out of sight, and then dashed into the shop to buy a muffin and a cup of hot chocolate. I wasn't particularly thirsty, but I needed something to warm my hands on.

"Wuu lie leeft?" I said through a mouthful of muffin.

The young wizard looked at me, totally confused. "Sorry, what did you say?"

I swallowed the rest of the muffin. "I said, 'would you like a leaflet'?"

"Definitely not!" He'd just noticed the photograph of Grandma on the front.

"It's about the election." I tried to push one into his hand.

"I don't care." He backed away. "That photo will give me nightmares."

"That's my grandmother you're talking about."

"In that case, my advice to you, is never grow old."

That set the pattern. For every two I gave out, I got one back again. And, I'd completely given up on the posters. Every time I put one up, someone came along and tore it down. I was getting nowhere fast. My pile of leaflets didn't seem to be getting any smaller. I had to come up with a plan.

Then I saw it.

No one need ever know.

I glanced around to ensure the twins couldn't see me, then I sidled slowly over to the bin. With my back to it, I felt for the opening, and then dropped the leaflets in.

Whoops!

Ten minutes later, the twins came back. They both still had a pile of leaflets.

"We're wasting our time," Pearl said.

"Nobody wants these." Amber shook the pile of leaflets.

"I had no problem getting rid of mine." I showed them my empty hands.

"How did you do it?"

"I just used my natural charm, obviously."

They both eyed me suspiciously.

"One of those muffins has gone." Amber pointed to the

shop window.

"Really?" I turned around to look. "Well, it definitely wasn't me. I've been too busy handing out leaflets."

"Yeah, we believe you," Pearl said. "Not."

***

Drake had booked a table at 'Blue', a restaurant in Candlefield. It wasn't one I'd heard of, but then I'd still only scratched the surface of the sup world. On arrival, I discovered that most of the exterior was in fact painted red: the walls, the door, the window frames, and even the sign. Colour me confused! See what I did there? Colour me—oh, never mind. My humour is wasted here.

We'd arranged to meet at eight, and it was now five-past. Surely he wasn't going to stand me up.

"Jill!" He suddenly appeared, out of breath. "I'm really sorry. Have you been waiting long?"

"No, I've only just arrived."

"I took Chief for a walk in the park, and he wouldn't come back when I called him."

"Oh dear." I laughed. "Now you know how it feels."

"It's just not like him. He's normally such an obedient dog."

"Yeah well. Dogs—they're unpredictable. Mine's depressed at the moment."

"Why's that?"

"His hamster won't talk to him. He's otherwise occupied."

"Let me guess." Drake grinned. "Book club?"

"How did you know?"

"It's the same at my place. Chief wanted a hamster. I

wasn't sure, but I went along with it. Then he started complaining because The Bard spent all of his time reading."

"The Bard?"

"That's the hamster's name. Don't ask. Anyway, The Bard has even started a book club."

"That's unbelievable. So has Hamlet."

"Hamlet?"

"Barry's hamster."

We both realised the absurdity of the conversation, and laughed.

"Have you been here before?" I asked.

"Yeah, a few times."

"I'm a little confused. Everything is red."

"The colour scheme works though; don't you think?"

"Yeah, but the name?"

"Blue? That's because they play blues here."

"Why didn't they call it 'blues' instead of 'blue'?"

"They did. The 'S' fell off. That seems to happen a lot in Candlefield. People just got used to calling it Blue, and the name stuck."

The food was excellent, and so was the service. The music? Whilst I was never going to be a big blues fan—it was okay. The restaurant wasn't too busy, so we had managed to get a quiet table. It was good to spend some time with Drake.

"How's the house hunting going?" I felt I should ask, although I hoped he might have changed his mind about finding a place in Washbridge.

"Not very well. I haven't made much progress so far."

"Oh dear, that's a shame." What do you mean:

hypocrite?

"But, I have a feeling my luck might be about to change."

"Why's that?"

"I was in Cuppy C the other day, and the twins asked about my house-hunting. I told them I was on the point of giving up, and your grandmother happened to overhear."

"Grandma?"

"She was there with friends. She said she might be able to help."

Oh no.

"Help how?"

"Apparently, she's expanded her business. It's a wool shop, isn't it?"

"Yeah, Ever A Wool Moment."

"She said she'd expanded into the empty shop next door. Apparently, there's a flat above the shop which she's had renovated, and is looking to let. That's great, isn't it?"

"Great!" I tried to sound enthusiastic.

Grandma must somehow have known that I didn't want Drake to live in Washbridge. She was messing with my head again.

"I'm going around there tomorrow to take a look at it. Would you like to come with me?"

"I'm sorry, but I can't. It's election day in Candlefield."

"Oh yes. I remember now. Your grandmother did say she wouldn't be at the flat, but that someone called Kathy would show me around."

Oh great! So, not only was Drake going to be living in Washbridge, but my sister, who knew nothing about him, was going to be showing him around the flat. It just got better and better!

"Kathy's my sister." I knew I had to tell him—it was going to come out anyway.

"Really?"

"Well my adoptive sister actually."

"Your grandmother never mentioned that."

"She's forgetful like that."

Chapter 19

When I left for work the next morning, Mr Ivers was sitting on the wall outside our flats.

"Morning, Jill," he said, barely looking up.

"Are you okay, Mr Ivers?"

"Yeah, I suppose so."

"Are you sure? You don't sound okay."

"Well, seeing as you asked—"

When would I ever learn?

"I'm feeling a bit down at the moment."

"Why's that?"

"You've probably noticed that I don't have a girlfriend."

There had been a short spell when Mr Ivers had been transformed into 'Ivy', the playboy, who'd had several girlfriends within the space of a week. But magic had been involved, and as soon as the spell had been reversed, he'd reverted to the pathetic creature now sitting in front of me. Poor old Mr Ivers; he wasn't what you'd call a looker, although the makeover the twins had given him had certainly improved his appearance. He had no charisma, and his *get up and go* had long since got up and gone. In short, he had absolutely nothing going for him.

"I'm sure there's someone out there for you somewhere."

"But where? I've tried everything. I've joined countless clubs and societies to try and meet someone. I've even tried online dating."

"How did that work out?"

"I went on a couple of dates, but they never contacted me again."

"What sort of things did you talk about on your dates?"

"Movies, mainly."

"That could be the problem. Not everyone is as keen on movies as you are."

"What about you, Jill?" he said. His eyes brightened for a moment. Oh no! Alarm bells were ringing. "I've always felt like you and I would make a good match. And, you don't seem to have a boyfriend. I thought maybe—"

"No. I—err—there is someone."

"I haven't seen you with anyone."

"No. They—he—sometimes works away—a lot—often."

"So you and I couldn't—"

"No. I'm sorry. I'm spoken for."

"Oh." He looked downcast again. I felt like I'd just told a young child there was no Santa Claus.

"I do have a suggestion, though."

"What's that?" He looked at me, hopefully.

"I happen to know of an exclusive dating agency which might be able to help you."

"I've tried dating agencies before."

"You won't have tried this one, and the owners just happen to be friends of mine." I felt in my pocket and took out the Love Spell card. "Here, take this. Give them a call, and tell them Jill Gooder recommended that you contact them. I'm sure you'll get the VIP treatment."

He looked at the card. "Do you really think they might be able to help?"

"I'm sure they will. What do you have to lose?"

"Okay, I will. Thank you."

As I drove to the office, I began to have second thoughts. What had I done? Milly, Lily, Tilly and Hilary had told me about their stringent vetting procedure. I wasn't sure Mr Ivers would get through *any* vetting procedure, particularly if there was a boredom threshold built into the test.

***

The Scoots were waiting for me when I arrived at the office. I hadn't been expecting them, and I could tell by their demeanour that something was wrong. Mrs Scoot looked as white as a ghost—if you'll pardon the pun. Mrs V had apparently given each of them a scarf, but that didn't appear to have helped.

"I know we don't have an appointment," Mr Scoot said. "But we hoped you might have time to see us."

"Yes, of course. Please come through." I led them into my office.

Winky was on at me as soon as I walked in.

"You'll have to wait for your food," I said under my breath.

He scowled, but I ignored him.

"Take a seat," I said. "Would you like a drink?"

They declined the offer.

"What's happened?"

"It's getting worse," Mr Scoot said. "We can't stay in that house another night."

"I won't go back there," Mrs Scoot said.

"Can you tell me what happened? Did you see something?"

"Objects were moving around, there were strange noises, doors opening and closing by themselves—"

"But you didn't actually see a ghost?"

"I don't know," Mrs Scoot said. "I was upstairs in the bedroom, looking in the mirror, when I thought I saw something behind me. But when I turned around, there was nothing there."

"The same thing happened to me when I was shaving," Mr Scoot said. "I bent over to rinse my face, and when I looked up, there was someone or some*thing* looking over my shoulder. But when I turned around, there was nothing there. We can't both be imagining things, can we?"

"I don't know," I admitted. "Why don't I stay there tonight, and see what I find? Something about this situation doesn't sit right with me. The best thing you can do is go and stay with someone. Do you have relatives close by?"

"My mother lives nearby," Mrs Scoot said. "We could stay with her for a while."

"In that case, why don't you go home and pack?"

"I can't go back there!" Mrs Scoot sounded panic-stricken.

"I'll go and get us a few things," Mr Scoot offered. "And then we'll go to your mother's."

I felt really sorry for the Scoots. They clearly loved that house, but were now too afraid to spend another night there.

I'd never liked scary movies; they always made me jump. Kathy absolutely loved them, and often used to drag me along with her. I think she enjoyed seeing me with my hands over my eyes during the scary bits. And, even though I now regularly talked to a ghost, I was still worried about spending the night at the Scoots' house.

Maybe I should have a talk with my mother first. If anyone should have the lowdown on hauntings, she should.

"You called?" My mother appeared at the other side of my desk.

"How do you do that?"

"I'm your mother. When you call, I come running—well more like floating, I suppose."

"But I was only *thinking* about calling you."

"Same thing in my book. What was it you wanted to talk to me about?"

I quickly brought her up to speed with the Scoots' case.

"Do you think it could be a ghost?" I said.

"It's possible, but I share your concerns. It sounds more like some sort of scam. I don't understand why so many houses on the same street would suddenly experience a haunting. Also, the fact that the vacated properties have been bought by an anonymous buyer is very suspicious."

"What would you suggest I do?"

"I think your idea to spend the night there is the right approach."

"But what if there *is* a ghost?"

"There's no reason for you to be afraid. You're a level three witch and more than a match for any ghost."

"I suppose so." I tried to appear confident, but deep down inside, I was terrified.

"Hey, you!" Winky said, after my mother had disappeared. "A cat could die of starvation in this office."

"You have enough fat reserves to keep you going for weeks."

"Cheek! You can talk."

"What do you mean?"

"I've noticed you're putting on the pounds. It must be all of those custard creams and blueberry muffins."

***

Not only was I facing the prospect of a night in a haunted house, but first I had an even scarier day in front of me. Today was election day in Candlefield, and I'd arranged to meet Grandma, Aunt Lucy and the twins at the Town Hall. If the result went against Grandma, my life would be a misery. Recent polls had shown Grandma was running neck and neck with Lance Boyle; it was too close to call.

"So you decided to come then?" Grandma said, when I arrived at the Town Hall steps.

"It's only just after eleven."

"Some of us have been up since six o'clock," she said, tapping her watch.

"I do have a business to run in Washbridge, you know. I had some clients to see."

"Oh, I'm *so* sorry. I didn't realise your silly little P.I. business was more important than my election campaign."

"I didn't say it was more important—"

"That's what it sounded like to me."

"Mother!" Aunt Lucy said. "Jill's doing the best she can. She's juggling two different worlds. Give her a break."

"Give her a break? How many times have I told her to stop messing about with the stupid human world, and to concentrate on what really matters here in Candlefield?"

That was rich coming from her, with her ever

expanding wool empire based in Washbridge. I bit my tongue; I was already in enough trouble without digging myself into an even deeper hole.

"Do you like our new outfits?" Amber said.

Normally, discussing clothes with the twins would have bored me senseless, but today I was glad of the distraction.

"They're very nice. What would you call that style exactly?"

"It's the very latest thing," Pearl said. "It's 'futuristic'."

"So, plastic is 'in', is it?" I stared at their skirts. "And what are those tops made from? It looks a bit like tin foil."

"Don't be silly." Amber laughed. "It's a revolutionary new fabric. Have a feel."

"I touched the hem of her top; it crinkled in my fingers which confirmed my suspicion that it really was made from some kind of tin foil.

"Very nice," I lied.

"They were very expensive," Pearl said.

"Well, I suppose Cuppy C is doing well."

"*We* didn't buy them." Amber laughed. "We got the guys to buy them for us."

"Where are your fellows anyway?" I said. "I haven't seen William and Alan for ages."

"Oh they're around. They have to work long hours to keep us in the style we've become accustomed to," Pearl said.

They both giggled.

Although they'd said it in jest, I suspected there was more than a grain of truth in their words. I rarely saw either of their fiancés these days, and they rarely went out together. Still, their relationships seemed to have lasted longer than any I'd managed so far. So, what did I know?

"I'm sorry to interrupt your ramblings." Grandma stepped between us. "But there is an election going on here today, in case you hadn't noticed."

"Sorry, Grandma," I said. "What would you like me to do?"

"I *would* have liked you to ensure I won this election, and if you'd done what I asked, and dug up dirt on Lance Boyle, then we'd be sitting pretty. But because you refused to use such tactics, we seem to be running neck and neck."

"I told you I wouldn't do anything underhand when you asked me to be your campaign manager."

"I seem to remember that you also told me the other campaign manager had agreed not to either, but that didn't pan out, did it?"

"I can't help it if he's a lying scum-bag."

Just then, I spotted Dexter Long. He gave me a wave. I ignored the low-life slime ball.

It turned out to be a very long day indeed. The twins had the good sense to go shopping; with a promise to return in the evening for the result. Aunt Lucy had conveniently remembered that she'd arranged to meet Lester, but she too had promised to return later. I would have dearly loved to get away too, but there was no chance of that happening. Grandma never took her eyes off me. She insisted that I sweet-talk everyone who was on their way in to cast their vote. I'm not sure that did much good because most people had already made up their mind. Most of those I spoke to had already decided to vote for Lance Boyle, but I didn't tell Grandma that.

The polls closed at ten o'clock by which time I was dead on my feet. Aunt Lucy had returned along with Lester and the twins. We were all waiting for the results to be announced. The count took far less time than it would have done in the human world because magic was employed. By ten-thirty, the two candidates, together with their campaign managers, were on the stage for the announcement. I looked down and saw Aunt Lucy, Lester and the twins standing at the front. They were looking at me as one might stare at a condemned man awaiting execution.

"I, Marmaduke Matthews, the Returning Officer for Candlefield, hereby announce the results of the election to the position of town councillor: Mirabel Marigold Millbright—one hundred and twenty thousand, one hundred and twenty-one votes."

There was applause all around the room. Surely Grandma had to win with so many votes? I glanced at her, but she was stony-faced.

"Lance Edward Boyle—" the returning officer continued. "One hundred and twenty thousand, one hundred and twenty-two votes."

The crowd erupted. My heart sank. She'd lost by one vote! One vote out of two hundred and forty thousand. I couldn't believe it.

The twins, Aunt Lucy and Lester joined us on stage.

"Well, Mother, you did your best. You can't get closer than that."

"I should have won easily," Grandma ranted. "If this

granddaughter of mine hadn't been so holier than thou with her election tactics, I would have won by a landslide."

"But, Mother, surely you wouldn't have wanted to win using underhand tactics, would you?"

"Of course I would! What good is losing, to anyone? Next time I run for election, I'll find a campaign manager who actually has a clue." With that she stomped off into the crowd.

"I think I'm in her bad books again," I said.

The twins laughed. "Oh well. It's not like you'll notice any difference."

"And besides," Aunt Lucy said. "It's probably for the best. Can you imagine what it would be like if your grandmother was on the Town Council?"

"But it was so close." I sighed. "Just one vote would have made the difference."

Aunt Lucy winked at me. "Good thing I voted for the opposition then."

Chapter 20

By the time I arrived at the Scoots' house, I was exhausted. The election had been an absolute nightmare, and Grandma wasn't likely to let me forget about it for some time to come. And the worst part? It was Aunt Lucy's vote which had lost Grandma the election. If she ever found out, she'd go ballistic. If I was a really horrible person, I would tell her, so as to deflect the blame away from me. What? Of course I wasn't going to. Probably not, anyway.

Palm Close looked normal enough, but it was quite dark because one of the street lights wasn't working. The Scoots had given me a key, so I let myself in and flicked on the light switch.
Nothing!
The power was out. It was dark and very cold. Fan—tas—tic! I found a pillow and blanket in the linen cupboard, then made my way into the living room where I settled down on the sofa. I wasn't nearly as cold once I was snuggled under the blanket. The house was remarkably quiet, and I soon felt my eyes closing. It had been a long, tiring day.

I woke with a start. It was three in the morning; I'd been asleep for several hours. But what had woken me? I heard a noise. It sounded like someone was moving around at the back of the house. I peeled back the blanket, climbed off the sofa, and made my way slowly towards the hallway. If it *was* a ghost, what was I supposed to do? What if it *wasn't* a ghost? What if it was criminals who were hell bent on getting the residents out of their homes? Why was I so worried? I was a witch! A level *three* witch! I knew plenty of spells; I could handle a few criminals or ghosts.

I heard another sound; this time from the kitchen. I crept forward and pushed open the door. I'm not sure who jumped the most: me or the woman on the other side of the door.

"Jill?" a familiar voice said.

"Mad?" I gasped. "What are *you* doing here?"

Madeline Lane was an old school friend of mine. Her nickname was Mad Lane.

"Never mind what *I'm* doing here," she said. "What are *you* doing here?"

"I'm a private investigator, remember? The people who live in this property hired me to find out what's going on in their house; they think it's haunted. Are you the one who's been scaring the residents out of their houses?"

"Is that really what you think of me? Wow! It's nice to know you hold me in such high regard."

"What am I supposed to think? Why else would you be here in the middle of the night?"

"It's complicated."

"That's all right, I've got all night."

"I know this is going to sound weird," Mad said. "But I'm actually a ghost hunter."

I laughed. "No, seriously, what are you doing here?"

"It's true. That's what I do. The librarian gig is just a cover. I moved back to Washbridge to hunt down ghosts."

"What do you mean 'hunt down ghosts'?"

"Exactly that, but before I get into it, there's something

else I should tell you."

"Go on."

"I know you're a witch."

"Don't be ridiculous." I laughed.

"You don't have to pretend with me, Jill. I know you're not supposed to tell humans, but I have special dispensation. I'm not exactly human myself."

"*O – kay*. So what are you then?"

"I'm what's known as a 'parahuman'."

"And what exactly is a *parahuman*?"

"It's someone who is essentially human, but who has extreme paranormal sensitivity. The bottom line is that I can see ghosts. I've always been able to. Don't you remember when we were kids, and people used to think I was weird?"

"Wasn't that because of the way you dressed?"

"That was part of it, I suppose. But I've always been able to see ghosts; I see them all the time. When I was a kid, I had no idea that other people *couldn't* see them; I just assumed everyone could. As I got older, I realised that it was just me, so I learned to keep quiet about it."

"How on earth did you get into ghost hunting?"

"I only recently started in the job. Before this, I was working in London. I had a lot of part-time jobs: bar work, waitressing, that kind of thing. I've never held down a job for more than six months – I usually ended up getting sacked because I didn't know when to keep my mouth shut. You know what I used to be like at school."

I did. Mad was always getting into trouble for shooting her mouth off – with the teachers, and with her parents.

"I drifted from one job to another," she continued. "On the same day as I lost my last job, I also discovered that my boyfriend was seeing my best friend."

"That must have stung."

"No kidding. I was at a pretty low ebb. I had no job, no money, and no boyfriend. And then, out of the blue, a ghost offered me a job. And yes, I know how weird that sounds. I'm so used to being around ghosts that I barely notice them, but when this one offered me a well-paid job, I didn't see that I had anything to lose. Mind you, I wasn't told exactly what the job would entail until much later. Before I started in the job, I had to go on a training course in GT."

"Gin and tonic?"

"You've got booze on the brain. No, it's the place where all the ghosts hang out. I can't remember its proper, official name; it's silly and posh-sounding, but everyone refers to it as Ghost Town—hence 'GT'. In the same way as you are able to move between the human world and the supernatural world, I can do a similar thing between the human world and GT."

"What's it like there?"

"Pretty much like the human world, except that everyone there is a ghost, apart from me and a few other ghost hunters."

"Are there many of you?"

"Not many. I've probably met another dozen or so."

"I still don't know why you came back to Washbridge."

"Not through choice." She grinned. "This is the last place I wanted to live. If you remember, I couldn't wait to get away from here when I left school. The ghost who recruited me didn't tell me I'd have to come back here. If he had, I probably would have turned down the job. But by the time I found out, I'd already gone through all the training. So here I am, back to my roots."

"Why do they want you to be based in Washbridge of all places?"

"It's a hotspot for supernaturals—"

"Sups, please."

"Sorry, I'm not up on all the terminology yet. Anyway, it's not just sups, it's ghosts too. There's some kind of bridge between Washbridge and the paranormal world. So I'm stuck here—which is just dandy."

"I can't get over how different you look compared to when you came to my office."

"You mean my 'librarian look'." She laughed.

When I'd known Mad at school, she'd been quite the 'wild child'. But when I'd seen her again recently, for the first time in years, she'd been wearing a woollen suit, her hair had been in a neat bun, and she'd told me she was working as a librarian. Now here she was, looking just like she used to: in cut off denim shorts, a low-cut vest top and hair which looked like she'd been pulled through a hedge backwards. This was more like the Mad I used to know.

"And, you're working as a librarian?"

"Yeah. What a joke! Again, not my idea. The powers-that-be decided all ghost hunters need a cover: librarians, civil servants, tax inspectors—"

Tax inspectors? Could Betty be a ghost hunter? Nah.

"So by day I'm a librarian but by night I'm a ghost hunter."

"And that's why you're here now?"

"Yeah. It's my job to capture ghosts who are up to no good in the human world."

"So a bit like a Rogue Retriever then?"

"A what?"

"It's something we have in the sup world. They have the job of bringing back rogue supernaturals from the human world. I occasionally work with one of them. She goes by the name of Daze."

"Yeah, that pretty much sounds like what I do, but with ghosts. This is only my third assignment. The intel I have is that there are a couple of ghosts who've been employed to scare the residents away from this street. As far as we can make out, the humans behind the scam are buying the vacant properties. Once they have possession of all of the houses in the street, we believe they're going to have them demolished, and build a shopping mall on the site. They can only go ahead with the development if they can obtain possession of all the properties."

"How did humans contract with ghosts in the first place?"

"They didn't. Not directly, at least. As far as I can make out, this scam was arranged via a third party—a parahuman."

"You mean someone with the same powers as you?"

"That's right. Not all parahumans are ghost hunters. Some make a living working with the 'bad' guys. Whichever parahuman arranged this probably has connections with the criminal fraternity in Washbridge. I doubt the people who are trying to buy up the properties know or care what methods are being used to drive the residents out. They certainly won't know it's ghosts."

"Have you actually seen the ghosts yet?" I said.

"No, I'd only just arrived when you came through the door, and made me jump."

"Sorry about that."

"That's okay. It's a good thing I didn't have Albert with me, though."

"Albert? Wasn't he that fierce dog you had when you were a kid?"

"Albert isn't fierce." She laughed.

"How can you still have the same dog after all these years?"

"He's a ghost."

"You have a ghost dog?"

"Yeah. That's another reason I took the job. I was undecided, but then they told me that Albert was waiting for me in GT. He's been there ever since he died."

"Have you been reunited with him?"

"Yeah. I'll eventually be able to bring him with me to Washbridge when I'm working on a job, but it'll take him a while to adjust because he's lived in GT for such a long time. It was fantastic to see him again after all this time. He hasn't changed."

"You mean he still bites people's heads off?"

"Given the chance, yeah." She laughed.

Chapter 21

"Here, take these." Mad passed me a pair of what looked like sunglasses.

"What are they?"

"Ghostvision glasses."

"They're *what*?" I laughed.

"You're going to need them. Remember, *I* can see ghosts, but you can't."

"I can see my mother's ghost."

"That's because she's attached herself to you. You won't be able to see other ghosts unless you wear these."

"They're not very attractive. Do you have them in other styles?"

"Just put them on."

I put on the silly glasses—it wasn't a great look. "What now?"

"Now we wait."

"What do we do when the ghosts turn up?"

"*We* don't do anything. *You* leave it to *me*."

I didn't argue. I had enough on my plate being a witch. I didn't want to have to deal with capturing ghosts.

"So, what's it like to be a witch?"

"It's pretty weird to be honest. I didn't even know I was one until recently when my birth mother died."

"That must have been pretty strange. I know I'm new to this job, but I've always been able to see ghosts, so it's not like it's that big a deal. I assume nobody knows you're a witch?"

"I'm not allowed to tell anyone—not even my sister."

"Why don't you show me some magic?" She laughed. "Do you have a wand?"

"No, I do *not* have a *wand*. What would you like me to show you?"

"I don't know—impress me."

"Okay then, what about—"

We both heard a noise coming from upstairs.

"Sounds like they're here." Mad stood up. "Stay behind me."

We both crept up the stairs. The noise was coming from the front bedroom, and it was getting louder. When we reached the landing, Mad turned to me, and indicated that we'd go in on three. She counted down using her fingers, then kicked open the door. Inside, there was a green glow coming from the far side of the room, and I could see two figures. Out of curiosity I looked over the top of the glasses. Without the aid of ghostvision, I couldn't see them at all.

The two ghosts looked startled.

"Okay, guys, the game's up," Mad shouted.

"You can see us?" one of the ghosts said.

"Of course I can see you. How else would I know you're so ugly?"

"She's a hunter!" the second ghost said. "Let's get out of here."

"Too late for that, boys." From somewhere, Mad produced a lasso which she threw over them. They immediately disappeared in a puff of smoke.

"Where did they go?" I gasped.

"They're back in GT."

This really was similar to what Daze did.

"So what happens now?"

"I file a report and they get thrown in jail. Job done."

"So the hauntings are over?"

"Yeah. This job really is a breeze. Pays well too. Look, I have to go, Jill. The paperwork is actually more difficult than catching the ghosts."

"I don't suppose I could come with you to GT, could I?"

"Sorry. GT is a no-go area for humans or supernaturals—err—sorry—I mean sups. But I imagine we'll bump into each other again."

"I hope so. It was nice to see the old Mad again."

"It's nice to *be* the old Mad again. I'm not keen on the librarian. I'll see you around, Jill. Bye."

"Bye, Mad."

And with that she was gone. Mission accomplished.

***

When I arrived at the office the next morning, Mrs V held out a parcel.

"It's for *him*." She gestured to my office.

I didn't need to ask who 'him' was. Sure enough the parcel was addressed to Winky, care-of my office.

"That must be the fur restorer." Winky snatched it from my hand, and tore open the package to reveal a jar of white ointment.

While he was struggling to remove the lid, I picked up the box and read the label.

"Have you seen the possible side-effects?"

"They always put that sort of thing on the label. It's just to cover themselves. It's nothing to worry about. After all, it's only fur restorer."

"Yeah, but there are some pretty scary—"

"Shush! Can't you see I'm busy?"

I watched as he tried to reach the miniscule bald spot.

"It's no use—I can't reach it. You'll have to do it."

"I'm not touching your bottom!"

"It's not on my bottom, it's on my back."

"I'm not sure I want to get that stuff on my fingers. I don't want to end up with hairy fingers."

"Here, use these." He passed me a pair of surgical rubber gloves.

"Where did you get those from?"

"I bought them yesterday. Just in case."

I put on the gloves, opened the jar and took a scoop of the gooey, white ointment.

"Are you sure about this, Winky? It smells horrible."

"Just get on with it!"

"Turn around then." I did it as quickly as possible, and then threw away the gloves. I just hoped it did the job.

The Scoots arrived just before lunchtime. It was great to have good news for them.

"I'm very pleased to tell you that you can move back into your house. You won't have any more problems."

"Did you find out what was happening?" Mr Scoot said.

"Just as we suspected, someone was trying to get the residents out of their houses, so they could raze the whole street to the ground, and build a shopping mall."

"What about the ghosts?" Mrs Scoot still looked worried.

"There never were any. It was just some elaborate hoax set up by the people wanting to buy the properties."

"That's terrible," Mrs Scoot said. "Why would anyone do such a thing?"

"There are some horrible people in this world, I'm afraid."

"You're absolutely sure we can move back in, and we won't be disturbed again?"

"You have my word. And what's more, your old neighbours will be moving back in too."

"How?"

"I had a quiet word with the criminals behind this scam, and suggested that they offer the houses back to the people they'd driven out. At a discount, of course."

"And they agreed?" said Mr Scoot.

"They did, once they realised that the game was up, and I threatened to take it to the police and the press."

"Thank you so much, Jill. You don't know how much this means to us."

"My pleasure." I started to walk them to the door.

"I play darts myself," Mr Scoot said, somewhat out of the blue.

"Darts?"

"Obviously not to your standard." He smiled.

I must have looked puzzled because he pointed at the trophy which Winky had put in the corner of the office.

"Oh, that thing? That isn't—err. I didn't—err." I spotted Winky out of the corner of my eye. He was grinning from ear to ear. "It's something I won ages ago. I don't play anymore."

"Still, something to be proud of?"

"Absolutely."

"Your trophy could do with a polish," Winky said, after they'd left.

"Oh shut up. Go tidy your eye patches."

***

I called in at Cuppy C with the intention of helping out for a couple of hours, but when I got there, the cake shop and tea room were both quiet. Instead, I helped myself to a cup of coffee and a blueberry muffin.

"How's Grandma?" I said.

"Need you ask?" Amber pulled a face.

"Yeah, she's even worse than usual." Pearl agreed.

"Hasn't she got over the election result yet?" I took a bite of muffin.

"What do you think? Every time we see her, she has another moan about it. She says you should have demanded a recount."

"Me? I didn't think it was my job to ask for a recount. *She* should have asked for one."

"She reckons that if there'd been a recount, she would have won."

"So, just to recap: everything is my fault."

"That's pretty much it," Pearl said.

"I should have realised."

"By the way, Jill." Amber glanced around to make sure she couldn't be overheard. "Who did you vote for?"

"Who do you think? Grandma, of course. I'm not stupid."

"We didn't," Pearl whispered.

"What?"

"We didn't vote for Grandma." Amber grinned.

"Why not?"

"Because if she'd won the election, it would have been terrible. It's bad enough having her as our grandma. If she was running Candlefield—can you imagine how bad that would be?"

"You won't tell Grandma, will you?" Pearl looked worried now.

"You'd better hope I don't. If she ever finds out that her granddaughters *and* her daughter voted for her opponent, I wouldn't want to be in your shoes. I'm the only one in her family who actually voted for her. Maybe I *should* tell her, then she'd be annoyed with you lot instead of me?"

"You can't do that! Please, Jill. Remember what she did to our ears? She'd do something even worse this time."

"I'll have to give it some thought. Oh, look! I seem to have finished my blueberry muffin."

"You can have another one—on the house," Pearl said. "I'll go and get it now."

"That's very kind of you. And another coffee wouldn't go amiss."

I'd no sooner taken a bite out of my second muffin than the door crashed open. All conversation in the tea room stopped, as in walked Ma Chivers, followed closely by Alicia and Cyril. Her eyes were blazing with anger as she stared at me.

"I thought I might find you here," she said.

"Hello, Ma."

"Don't call me, Ma. My name is Mrs Chivers."

"Oh—right—sorry. Is there something I can help you with, *Mrs Chivers*?"

"There's nothing *you* can help *me* with, young lady. But, as I mentioned when I visited your office, there's certainly something I could help you with. Do you see this young witch?" She gestured towards Alicia.

I glanced at my nemesis who scowled back at me.

"This young woman has had the benefit of my guidance

for some time now, and do you see how she's progressed?"

"I hear she's very good at poisoning people."

Alicia looked as though she was about to strike me, but Ma Chivers put out an arm and held her back.

"I'm a reasonable woman," Ma Chivers said.

I doubted that somehow, but now wasn't the time to contradict her.

"So I'm going to give you a second chance, which is not something I do very often. I'm going to invite you once again to come under my tutelage. Your grandmother's days are numbered. Her power is in decline. She can't even get elected to the town council! So, if you do have ambitions to progress as a witch, you really have only one choice. I'll ask you one last time: Will you come and study under my guidance?"

Her eyes burned into me. Alicia's eyes burned into me. Even Cyril's eyes burned into me.

Out of the corner of my eye, I could see Amber and Pearl who looked as terrified as I felt. My mouth was so dry I could barely speak, but I managed to swallow, and then said, "I'm sorry, Mrs Chivers, but I'd prefer to stay with my grandmother."

She pushed the table to one side, and got right in my face. For a moment, I feared for my life.

"Make a note of today's date, and be sure to remember it." She spat the words. "This is the day you made the biggest mistake of your life."

With that, she stormed out of the shop, leaving overturned tables and chairs in her wake.

On her way out, Alicia turned to face me, then drew a finger across her throat.

Chapter 22

Mrs V had her back pressed up against the door to my office, and was brandishing a large knitting needle.

"Don't go in there, Jill. Whatever you do, don't go in there!"

"What's the matter?"

"There's some kind of wild animal inside. I saw it when I went in to feed the cat, but I managed to get out before it could attack me."

Mrs V liked the occasional tipple. I'd seen the results of that once before when she and Grandma had had a night out on the tiles. It had involved boomerangs and sailors, if I remembered correctly. Perhaps she'd been at the bottle again?

"Are you sure about this, Mrs V?"

"Of course I am! It tried to eat me. It's all hairy and horrible."

"Okay, well let me just have a quick look—"

"No! It's far too dangerous." She stood her ground.

"I promise to be careful. And besides, I need to check on Winky."

"Oh, forget him."

"If there *is* a wild animal in there, Winky will be terrified."

"Okay, but be quick. And be careful." She stepped aside.

I slowly pushed open the door, and peered inside. I couldn't see anything. And I couldn't hear anything—not even Winky.

"Be careful, Jill," Mrs V said.

"It's okay." I crept inside and closed the door behind

me. I had one hand on the door handle—just in case I needed to make a quick exit. I still couldn't see anything. Maybe Mrs V *had* been drinking. Then suddenly, something small and hairy jumped up onto my desk.

"Get back!" I said.

"Don't just stand there!" a familiar voice said. "Help me!"

"Winky?"

"Who did you think it was?"

"What happened to you?"

Winky had been transformed into what looked like a miniature Old English Sheepdog. His fur was so long that he looked like a giant ball of wool. If he hadn't spoken to me, I wouldn't have known which was his front-end and which his back-end.

"What do you think happened? That stupid ointment happened!"

"Did you follow the instructions?"

"Of course I did. Well, more or less."

"What do you mean *more or less*?"

"I may have put on a *little* bit more than the instructions recommended."

"How much more?"

"The whole jar. I rubbed it all over my body; I figured it would prevent any other bald spots appearing."

"You idiot! Why on earth would you do that?"

"Never mind the lecture. What are you going to do about it?"

"What do you expect me to do?"

"Clip my fur."

"I don't know the first thing about clipping fur."

"You don't know anything about being a P.I., but—"

"Enough of the cheek!" Why did everyone keep saying that?

"Hurry up! I can't let anyone see me looking like this. What if Bella tries to contact me on Skype? I've stayed away from the window all morning in case she spotted me. You have to help me. And you have to do it now!"

"But I don't have any clippers."

"You've got scissors, haven't you?"

"It'll take forever to cut off all of that fur using scissors."

"Well then, the sooner you get started, the sooner it'll be done."

Two and a half hours later, I was completely exhausted. There was fur all over the desk and the floor. My fingers were sore from having to cut through so much of it.

"That's not bad at all," Winky said, admiring his reflection in the mirror. "You've done a good job there."

"Why, thank you, sir."

"Maybe you should consider giving up this P.I. lark, and set up as a cat trimmer?"

***

"It's not right, Jill," Mrs V said. She was still upset about Winky and the fur situation. "No animal's fur should grow so quickly. He must be possessed or something. Do you think he's a werecat?"

"I'm sure he's not. It was just a mix-up with the treatment I'd bought for his fur. Everything's okay now apart from my fingers." I showed her my hand. "Look, they're really sore where I've been using the scissors."

"I don't know why you don't get rid of that stupid cat.

I've told you before, he's a liability."

"Everything's back to normal now."

"Nothing's *normal* when it comes to that cat."

Just then, the outer door opened, and a little head appeared around it.

"Gertie?"

"Hi, Jill. Is it okay for me to come in?"

"Yes, of course. Come in."

I could see that she'd been crying; her eyes were red and puffy. "This is Mrs V, Gertie."

"Hello, Mrs V."

"Hello, young lady. Would you like a scarf? I have plenty for you to choose from." Mrs V opened the cupboard. Gertie was obviously taken aback by the variety and colour of scarves available. "Help yourself to one, dear. You can have some socks too, if you'd like."

After she'd chosen a nice yellow scarf and matching socks, we made our way through to my office.

"Is that your cat?" Gertie said.

"Yes, that's Winky."

"I like his fur."

"Thank you, young lady," Winky said. "I rather like it myself."

"He's only got one eye," Gertie couldn't stop staring at him.

"Yes, but he's still rather handsome, don't you think?"

"I guess so."

I shooed Winky off the desk and invited Gertie to sit down. "What can I do for you? Have you started at your new school?"

"Yes, two days ago. That's why I'm here. It's not going very well."

"What's wrong?"

"I haven't made any friends, and no one likes me. I was going to run away this morning—back to Candlefield, but then I remembered you said I could come and see you if things weren't going well. So here I am."

I'd hoped that once Gertie had started at her new school, things would click into place. It never occurred to me that she'd actually turn up at my office.

"Why don't I come to school with you—just for one day—to help you settle in?"

"They won't let you stay at school with me."

"Not normally, but you and I are witches, remember. If we put our heads together, I'm sure we can come up with a way that I can be at school with you without anyone knowing. And then, maybe I can give you a few pointers which will make things better."

"What kind of pointers?"

"I won't know until I get there, but I'm willing to give it a go if you are."

"I'm not sure." She sounded unconvinced.

"What do you have to lose?"

"I guess. When?"

"How about tomorrow? I'll meet you outside your house in the morning, and we'll go to school together. We'll show them what witches are made of."

By the time she left, Gertie was looking a little happier with life.

"Is she going to be okay?" Mrs V said.

"I think so. She's just moved to the area and is the new girl in school. She was a little upset, but I think I've managed to reassure her."

"You're good with children, aren't you, Jill?" Mrs V smiled. "It's about time you got married and had some of your own."

"Yeah, I think I'll pass on that one for the time being."

My phone rang and I was pleased for the distraction. I shuffled through to my office, away from Mrs V and her plans for my nuptials.

It was Jack Maxwell.

"Hi, Jack. How's things?"

"Jill. Sorry I haven't been in touch recently. I've been a bit busy. Look, the reason I'm calling is that there's a policemen's ball in a couple of weeks' time—"

"A policemen's ball? Seriously?" I laughed. "I didn't realise there were such things. I thought they only existed in comedy sketches."

"It's real, I promise you. Anyway, I just wondered if you'd like to accompany me?"

"You mean like on a date?"

"Err—well—err—" he blustered. "Yes, I suppose so."

"But wouldn't you rather take your paranormal consultant?"

"Deirdre has resigned. It came totally out of the blue."

"Why?"

"She said it was because she'd seen a ghost."

"But surely, that was her job, wasn't it? Seeing ghosts, I mean. I thought she could talk to them?"

"I really don't understand it. She said something about *this* ghost being a *real* one, and then she handed in her resignation and left."

"How very peculiar."

Good job, Mum! I owed her a few custard creams for that.

"So, what do you say? Are you up for the policemen's ball?"

"Sure, why not?"

"There's one thing I ought to mention," he said. "Every year there's a competition for the best couple."

"How do you mean?"

"Dancing partners. Deirdre was going to be my partner before she upped and left. I thought I might have to drop out, but then I remembered you said you had medals for dancing. I did get that right, didn't I?"

"Medals? For dancing? Err—yeah—dozens of them."

"That's great. I won the competition at my old stomping ground, three years on the trot. I'd like to think I could repeat that here in Washbridge. So it's a date then?"

"Err—yeah, it's a date. Bye, Jack."

***

Mrs V poked her head around the door.

"The colonel and Sir Cuthbert are here. Can you see them, Jill?"

My heart sank. I'd been dreading this moment. As much as I loved the colonel, he and Sir Cuthbert were the last people I wanted to see. I'd let them both down really badly. I'd accused Lady Phoebe of stealing her own vase *and* of having an affair with her gardener. What had I been thinking? Still, I had to face the music sooner or later, so I might as well get it over with.

"Yes, show them in, please."

Just as I'd expected they both looked extremely angry.

"Colonel, Sir Cuthbert, please take a seat, gentlemen. Can I just start by saying how sorry I am for what I said to

Lady Phoebe? It was unforgivable."

The two men sat stony-faced for a long moment, but then turned to face one another, and laughed.

Huh?

"It's all right, Jill," Sir Cuthbert said. "This whole affair has given us quite a good laugh. The idea that Phoebe and Roger Tyler were having an affair—priceless!"

"I don't know what I was thinking."

"Don't worry about it. All's well that ends well. The vase is back where it belongs, and we've even got the serpent plate back."

"You got the plate back as well?"

"Yes. As soon as Terry Brown found out that the one in his possession had been stolen, he insisted on returning it to us. I was happy to reimburse him the money he'd paid for it. He's a good chap. Salt of the Earth. Which is more than I can say for that scoundrel, Roger Tyler."

"He'll get what's coming to him," I said. I was feeling much better now.

"The police believe he had an accomplice, but no one seems to know who she is."

"It was a she?" I tried to sound surprised.

"According to Detective Maxwell, they suspect a woman may also have been involved, but she appears to have fled the scene—leaving Roger Tyler to carry the can. Anyway, to the reason I'm here. I believe I owe you some money, young lady."

"No, no. I couldn't possibly accept payment. Not after what happened."

"Look here, we hired you to find the vase, and find the vase you did. So I insist on paying you."

"That's very kind. And thank you for being so

understanding."

After the two men had left, Winky jumped onto my desk.

"I don't know how you do it," he said.

"What?"

"How did you get away with that? If that had been me, I would have sued your backside."

He was right. I'd really lucked out this time. It was only when Daze had mentioned Mona Lisa that I'd remembered the article in The Bugle. Someone had created an exact duplicate of one of the statues in the museum. The curators had found the two of them side by side. No one knew where the second one had come from. It was identical in every way.

I'd dismissed the article as nonsense at the time, but then when Daze had told me about Mona Lisa, I realised what had happened. She'd captured Mona Lisa in the museum, just after she'd made the duplicate, and before she could take away the original.

Mona Lisa had also been working with Roger Tyler. She'd duplicated the serpent plate, the original of which had eventually been bought by Terry Brown. After that success, they'd become more ambitious and had planned to steal the vase. Roger Tyler had taken it back to his place; Mona Lisa was supposed to meet him there to make the duplicate which Tyler would then have taken back to the house. But, in the meantime, Mona Lisa had been arrested by a Rogue Retriever—our very own Daze. Poor old Roger Tyler was left holding the baby or, in this case, the vase.

Lady Bunty believed she'd seen Lady Phoebe in

Winminster, but she'd actually seen Mona Lisa, who had used the 'doppelganger' spell while she sold the serpent plate.

Once I'd worked it all out, it was quite simple for me to use the same 'doppelganger' spell to make myself look like Mona Lisa. It had worked a treat. Roger Tyler had fallen for it, hook, line and sinker. After my meeting with him, I was able to tell Jack Maxwell where and when he would find the vase and the thief.

Job done!

Chapter 23

I'd arranged to meet Gertie at the end of her street. As I waited for her to appear, my phone rang.

"Jill? It's Hilary from Love Spell."

"Oh, hi. How's business?"

"Improving, thanks to you. We've stopped using Kaleidoscope, so hopefully things will get back to normal pretty soon, and then we can pay you some money."

"That would be nice."

"Anyway, the reason I called—"

I had a feeling I already knew. "Look, I'm sorry, Hilary. I know I shouldn't have sent him to you, but—"

"Sent who?"

"My neighbour, Mr Ivers. Isn't that why you're calling?"

"Oh yes, Mr Ivers. He said you'd referred him to us."

"I know he's probably not suitable, and he's unlikely to get through your vetting procedure, but he was so miserable—"

"No really, Jill, he's absolutely fine."

"He is?"

"Yes, he fits the criteria perfectly."

I was gobsmacked. "Are we talking about the same Mr Ivers?"

"The movie buff?"

"Yes that's him."

"You'd be surprised how many of the witches on our books have an interest in movies. In fact, Amber used to be registered with us at one time."

"Did she, really?"

"Didn't she tell you?"

"No, she didn't."

"She was on our books for quite some time, but I'm afraid we were never able to match her up with anyone suitable. Maybe, if your neighbour had been on our books back then? Who knows? Then, of course Amber met William, and cancelled her membership."

Amber and Mr Ivers? I'd have paid good money to see that.

"If it wasn't about Mr Ivers, why *did* you call?"

"I noticed that your profile is still on our books, and I was wondering whether you wanted me to remove it or if you'd like me to leave it on there and have us try to match you with someone?"

"I hadn't really thought about it. How much would it cost?"

"Nothing. Call it a gift for services rendered."

"Really? Well, in that case, why not?"

Gertie was walking towards me. She did *not* look happy.

"Morning, Gertie."

"Morning." It was more a groan than a greeting.

"How do you usually get to school?"

"There's a school bus. The bus stop is just down the road."

"Come on then, let's go catch it."

"Only kids are allowed on it. I thought you'd take your car and meet me there."

"No, I want to go with you. If I use the 'shrink' spell, you can pop me into the breast pocket of your blazer."

"Oh, okay then."

At least that brought a smile to her face.

"Be gentle though."

"I will," she promised.

I shrank myself, and waited for Gertie to pick me up. It was the first time anyone had held me in their hand; it felt weird and scary, but it was actually quite cosy once I was in her pocket. I peeped over the top every now and then, being careful not to let anyone see me. As we waited at the bus stop, I noticed several different groups of kids; they were all chatting to one another. Gertie was all by herself.

"Haven't you made friends with anyone yet then?" I whispered.

"No."

I noticed one of the other girls giving Gertie a strange look, so I stopped talking. I didn't want anyone giving her a hard time for being the crazy girl who talked to herself.

Gertie was the last one to get on the bus. There were no empty seats, although a few of them were only taken up with backpacks. No one seemed in any hurry to move their bag to let Gertie sit down.

"I've got an idea," I whispered.

Suddenly, all the girls on the bus looked up, and several of them moved their backpacks off the seats. Gertie looked puzzled, but walked to the nearest one and sat down. The girl next to her didn't speak; she just stared and smiled at Gertie.

When the bus pulled up outside the school gates, we were the first off.

"What happened just now?" Gertie looked puzzled.

"I cast an 'illusion' spell. The other kids thought you were Tom West from Game On."

"Who from What?"

"Come on, Gertie. You'll have to get up to speed with human music. Tom West is in Game On—the biggest boy band of the moment."

"I've never heard of him. No wonder everyone was staring at me. Do they still think I'm Tom West?"

"No. I reversed that spell, and then cast a 'forget' spell, just as we were getting off the bus. They won't remember a thing about it."

"I want the other kids to like me for who I am. Not because they think I'm lead singer with a boy band."

"Drummer, actually."

She rolled her eyes.

"You're right. It was a stupid idea. I'm sorry. Come on let's get inside."

It was the same school I'd attended when I was a kid, and I hadn't much liked it back then. From what I could see, nothing had really changed. It still had that same smell about it: chalk and sweaty PE kits.

"Which is your classroom?" I whispered.

"This one on the left. My desk is on the front row. It was the only one free."

We were about to go into the classroom when Gertie stopped dead in her tracks.

"Oh no! I've just remembered; I was supposed to read several pages of my history book last night. I forgot all about it. And there's a test this morning."

I pulled her to one side. "Have you got the book with you?"

"Yes, it's in my bag."

"Get it out."

"But it's too late." She took out the book anyway.

"No it isn't. Do you know the 'speed read' spell?"

"Yeah, I think so, but I've never actually used it. We weren't allowed to in my school in Candlefield—the teachers could tell if anyone did."

"Well you're in Washbridge now, and no human is going to know. Quick, cast the spell."

"Okay I'll try." She closed her eyes for just a few seconds. "Okay, I've done it."

"Now read the passage."

"I'm not sure I can do this, Jill."

"Yes you can. Have faith. Go on."

She looked down at the book, and I could see her eyes darting left and right as she flicked through the pages. Within a matter of seconds, she'd read all ten pages.

"See?"

"That was brilliant!" she said. "I don't know why I didn't think of that before."

"Can you remember what you read?"

"Yeah, all of it."

"Brilliant! Let's go in then."

Just as Gertie had said, her desk was right at the very front of the classroom. All of the other kids were chatting to one another, except for the girl at the desk next to Gertie's. She looked even more nervous than Gertie.

"Right, boys and girls, that's enough. Everyone to their desk, please. No more talking." The teacher, Miss Badland, was a real battle-axe. "I assume you've all read the section which I set for homework last night." As she spoke, she walked around the classroom, handing a sheet of paper to everyone. "In a moment, I'll tell you to turn over the test paper. It's multiple choice, so there's no excuse for running out of time. For every correct answer you will get one mark. For every incorrect answer you will get one mark deducted."

"But, Miss, that's not fair," a voice shouted from the back.

"Be quiet, Jordan. It's perfectly fair. It will show who has actually read and understood the passage, and who is just guessing."

"Still don't think it's fair, Miss."

The girl at the next desk glanced across at Gertie. She looked absolutely petrified, and I suspected she'd forgotten to do her history homework too.

"Right," Miss Badland said. "You may begin. You have thirty minutes."

The test underway, the teacher took a paperback out of her bag, and began to read. A cozy mystery, I think.

The kids turned over their test papers, and began ticking boxes. Gertie sped through hers in a matter of minutes; she obviously knew all of the answers.

"I think your friend is struggling," I whispered.

Gertie glanced at the girl at the next desk. She looked really scared and was shaking her head. Without any prompting from me, Gertie checked the teacher wasn't looking, and then reached over and picked up the girl's test paper. She quickly went through it, ticking all the answers, and then passed it back. The girl beamed and mouthed the words 'Thank you'.

When the thirty minutes were up, the teacher told the kids to put down their pens, then she collected the test papers. As Gertie was leaving the classroom, someone tapped her on the shoulder. She turned around to see the girl who'd been sitting next to her.

"Thanks ever so much for that," the girl said. "I thought I was dead."

"That's okay."

"My name's Julia."

"Gertie."

"I was just going to go to the cafeteria. Do you want to come with me?"

"Yeah, that would be great, thanks."

So far, so good. Gertie seemed to have found herself a new friend in Julia. School meals had improved dramatically since I was there. We used to be served slop, but today's meal smelled really good. Not that I was likely to find out because I was stuck in Gertie's pocket. I had hoped she'd realise I'd be hungry, and would sneak me something to eat, but she was so busy talking to her new friend that she'd apparently forgotten all about me. It was only after we left the cafeteria, while Julia was in the loo, that I managed to catch Gertie's attention.

"Hey! You haven't forgotten me, have you?"

"Sorry, Jill. Yes, I had. Julia and I have been busy talking."

"I know. And eating too. I'm starving in here."

"I'm sorry. If I'd realised, I could have given you some of my muffin. It was delicious."

"Was it *really*? How very nice for you."

Julia returned, so I popped my head back down inside the pocket. It was starting to get really hot and sweaty in there.

As Gertie and Julia made their way to the lockers, a boy shouted, "Hey, new girl, come over here."

"Ignore him," Julia said. "That's Bradley. He's horrible."

"Hey, new girl. Are you deaf? I said, come over here."

I could tell Gertie wasn't sure what to do, but eventually she walked over to the boy who was standing next to an open door.

"There's something in here I want to show you. Come and have a look."

"Don't do it," I whispered. I daren't say it any louder.

"What is it?" Gertie said.

"Look—down there."

She bent over to look. "I can't see anything," she said. "It's too dark."

"Down there!"

The next thing I knew we were tumbling head over heels. He'd pushed her into the cupboard, which was pitch black inside.

"Let me out!" She banged on the door.

"Gertie," I said. "Relax, it's okay."

"But he won't let me out."

"Stupid new girl," the boy shouted from outside the cupboard.

Gertie pushed hard against the door, but it was obviously locked.

"Is there a light switch, Gertie?"

She felt around, and eventually found one.

"It's not working. What shall I do? I can't be late for my next lesson."

"Don't worry. We'll figure something out."

"Let her out, Bradley." I heard someone say; it sounded like Julia.

"Why should I?"

"If you don't, I'm going to tell the teacher."

I was thrilled to hear Gertie's new friend sticking up for her. It couldn't have been easy for her to stand up to Bradley; he looked like a bit of a thug.

"Alright, keep your hair on. I'll let her out."

"Quick, Gertie," I said. "Shrink yourself."

"What?"

"Do as I say. Shrink yourself now. And make sure you shrink your clothes with you."

"But what about you?"

"Take me out of your pocket first."

She placed me gently on the floor.

"Hurry up! Before he opens the door!"

She cast the 'shrink' spell. Now, we were *both* tiny.

"Quick," I said. "Follow me."

As soon as the door opened, we rushed, unseen, past Bradley and Julia.

"Where are you, new girl?" Bradley said, obviously confused.

"Gertie, where are you?" Julia said.

"Quick," I whispered. "Change yourself back to full size and put me back in your pocket."

Gertie reversed the spell, and popped me back in her pocket. Then she walked up behind Bradley, and tapped him on the shoulder.

"Are you looking for me?"

Bradley turned around and did a double take. So did Julia.

"How did you get out?" he said.

"I have magical skillz." Gertie grinned.

"That's my girl!" I said quietly to myself.

Julia beamed at Gertie, and the two of them walked off, leaving Bradley shaking his head in disbelief.

Chapter 24

Gertie was much happier and relaxed in the first lesson of the afternoon, but when it ended, she seemed to flag again.

"What's wrong?" I whispered.

"It's sports day. I hate sports."

"You'll be okay."

"It's track and field. I hate all of that stuff."

"Gertie," a teacher wearing a tracksuit shouted. "We're one short for the relay team. You'll have to take the last leg."

"But, Sir. I'm not really—"

"You're the only one available. You'll take the last leg."

It was the annual sports day, so the rest of the afternoon was filled with all manner of sports and track events. The school had four house teams; Gertie was in Trueman. As the afternoon wore on, it became obvious that it would be a two horse race to determine which house would win the cup. By the time it came to the last event of the day, the relay, Trueman house were level on points with Gilbert house.

"This is terrible," Gertie said. "Everything depends on this race, and I have to run the last leg. I'll come last for sure."

"Don't panic." I tried to reassure her. "Have you ever used the 'faster' spell?"

"Yeah, once I think."

"Can you remember it?"

"I think so."

"Good. When you cast it, make sure you don't give it too much power—you don't want to make it too obvious.

Okay?"

"I guess so."

"Good. Look, I can't come out on the track with you."

"But, Jill—"

"You'll be okay. Pop me on the window sill so I can see out. Just before you receive the baton, cast the spell and everything will be fine."

"What if I lose? Everyone will hate me."

"You won't lose—not if you use the spell."

I was perched on the window sill next to an old pair of socks which Gertie had placed there for me to hide behind—they smelled awful. The window was rather dirty; I had to wipe a small area clean, so I could see outside. The competitors were taking their places. I could see Gertie standing at the last changeover point. Moments later, the starter fired the pistol, and off they went.

It was a mixed event. The first and third legs were to be run by boys, and the second and last legs by girls. By the end of the first leg, all four teams were neck and neck. By the end of the second, two of the runners were out in front; one of those was Gertie's team. Approaching the end of the third leg, Gertie's team were trailing in second place. She looked really nervous, and I prayed that she could remember the spell. Whatever happened, she couldn't afford to drop the baton. Her team mate held it out, and Gertie grabbed it first time. Then she set off at such a pace that I knew the spell had worked. It was incredible: one moment she was ten yards behind the leader, and the next she'd overtaken her, and was at the finish line.

Everyone looked astonished. Her three team mates

came rushing over; they were all cheering and jumping up and down with excitement. Gertie looked thrilled.

The announcement came over the loudspeaker: *"The winner of the final event is Trueman house. Which means that this year's sports trophy goes to – Trueman house"*.

All of the kids in Trueman house cheered and rushed down onto the track. They surrounded Gertie. Two young men picked her up and put her on their shoulders. She was beaming. I had a feeling that Gertie would be much more popular at school from now on, at least among those in Trueman house.

Once we were back outside her home, Gertie said, "Jill, thank you ever so much."

"Will you be okay now?"

"Yes, I think so. Julia is really nice. She's invited me around to her house at the weekend, and I said she can come to mine. Maybe I'll get some of my friends from Candlefield over, and they can meet her."

"Why don't you leave that for a while? Get to know Julia first, and see if you can make a few more friends here before you bring your other friends over."

"Yeah, you're probably right."

"So, do you think you'll be okay at school now?"

"Yeah, it was great today! Did you see what happened when I won the relay race?"

"I did. You were fantastic." It was so good to see her smiling. "Would you put me down onto the floor now, please?"

She did, and I reversed the 'shrink' spell. It felt good to be full size again, but I was absolutely starving.

"Thanks again, Jill."

"No problem. If you have any more problems, you know where I am. Just give me a shout."

***

It was the weekend that I'd promised to look after Aunt Lucy's house. She and Lester had left at the crack of dawn, and she'd given me a key. I'd promised to go over there early morning, and to stay for the weekend. It would be nice to relax for a change. I planned to catch up on some reading, and to generally chill out. Aunt Lucy had promised she'd get in some blueberry muffins and custard creams.

I was in the bedroom of my flat, packing an overnight bag, when I heard something. Was my mother stealing the custard creams again? I crept through to the living room. From nowhere, a figure jumped out in front of me. It was a man dressed in a tacky, blue catsuit. He was overweight with a beer belly. The catsuit looked terrible on him. But enough of my fashion critique. He pulled out a wire net similar to the one I'd seen Daze use, and before I could say or do anything, he'd thrown it over me.

Moments later, I was standing in a prison cell. I recognised my surroundings; I'd been there before with Daze when she'd captured a Rogue and brought him back to Candlefield. But why was I in prison? The beer-bellied, catsuited man was on the other side of the bars.

"What do you think you're doing?" I yelled. "Let me out of here!"

He ignored me, and walked out of the cell block. In the cell to the right of mine was a young male vampire.

"What are you in for, sweetheart?" he said.

"I'm not in for anything, and I'm not your sweetheart. This is a mistake."

"Yeah, course it is." He laughed. "That's what they all say."

"It's true! I haven't done anything wrong."

"Tell it to the authorities. I've tried that one, myself. Never worked for me."

"But it's true. I was in my flat, minding my own business. I'm not a Rogue."

"Hmm, you look a bit *'roguish'* to me, sweetheart."

Cheek!

"Let me out of here!" I shouted. "There's been a mistake." I rattled the bars.

Hold on. What was I thinking? I could just shrink myself and walk out of there. I cast the spell, but nothing happened.

"You're not trying to use magic, are you?" the vampire laughed.

"What's it to you?"

"You're wasting your time, sweetheart. They've got anti-magic systems in place. Nothing will get you out of here."

"We'll see about that." I cast the 'power' spell, so that I'd be able to bend the bars apart. But they wouldn't budge. I tried every spell I could think of, but nothing worked. What was I supposed to do now? I slumped down onto the bench, which was in one corner of the cell, and waited.

It was almost two hours later when the cell-block door opened again, and a familiar face entered. It was Maxine Jewell.

"Maxine," I said. "It's me, Jill Gooder. Do you remember me?"

"I know who you are."

"There's been a mistake. Someone brought me here from Washbridge and locked me up."

"Yes. That's their job. They retrieve Rogues from the human world."

"But I'm not a Rogue! I haven't done anything wrong. You know who I am."

"I know there's a warrant out for your arrest." She waved a piece of paper in front of me.

"For what? What am I supposed to have done?"

"That's not important right now. You'll have your day in court."

"What do you mean 'my day in court'? Surely I'm allowed to know what I am being accused of?"

"All in good time."

"When will my court appearance be?"

"Probably tomorrow. Maybe the day after. Who can say?"

"I'm meant to be housesitting for my aunt."

"You should have thought of that before you transgressed."

"I haven't *transgressed*. I haven't done anything wrong. Check the paperwork; there's obviously been a mistake."

"Just be quiet, Gooder, or I'll have to add a charge of disruption."

"*Disruption*? How about *false imprisonment*?"

"Yes, yes. Tell it to the judge." With that, she left.

"I can recommend a good lawyer, sweetheart," the vampire said.

"I don't need a lawyer. I haven't done anything wrong."

"You'd better have one with you when you go to court, or you'll get sent down for ever and a day."

"They can't do that."

"I wouldn't bank on it."

Later that morning, a werewolf appeared in the cell to the left of mine. He'd been brought in by another Rogue Retriever. The werewolf seemed quite relaxed about the whole thing. He was clearly used to being imprisoned. The only other person I saw all day was the guard who brought us what was laughingly referred to as dinner.

By eleven o'clock that night, there was still no sign of anyone coming to my aid. According to my new friend, the vampire, the next court session wouldn't be until Monday morning. Fantastic!

I was on the bench, trying to get some sleep when the door to the cell-block burst open.

"You can't go in there!" I heard Maxine Jewell's voice.

"Don't be ridiculous, Jewell." It was Daze. "Jill, are you okay?"

"Not really. I don't know why I'm here."

"You shouldn't be. As Maxine Jewell knows full well."

"There's a warrant for her arrest," Jewell shouted.

"That warrant is fake. It was an Unlicensed Operator who brought her here, and I suppose you paid him his bounty?"

"Well—err—yes," she stammered.

"Well then, you're an idiot. If you can't tell the difference between a licensed Rogue Retriever, and an Unlicensed Operator by now, then it's time you retired. Look at this paperwork; it's obviously forged." She thrust it into Maxine Jewell's hand. "Now let her out!"

"I can't do that."

"If you don't let her out within the next two minutes, I'll make sure everyone knows that you were taken in by an Unlicensed Operator."

Jewell hesitated, but then walked over to my cell and unlocked the door. "Come on then, hurry up. We need this cell."

I was so angry, I could have strangled her, but Daze ushered me out of the police station.

"Thanks, Daze. I thought I was going to be in there until Monday."

"It's absolutely ridiculous," she said. "There are more and more of these Unlicensed Operators around. They fabricate warrants, but usually the police have enough about them to realise they're fake, and don't pay out on them. I think Maxine deliberately turned a blind eye in your case. She seems to have it in for you for some reason."

"Tell me about it."

"Shall I come back with you to Washbridge?"

"No, I've promised to look after Aunt Lucy's house while she and Lester are away for the weekend."

"Are you sure you're okay?"

"Yeah, I'm fine now. Thanks, Daze."

I made my way over to Aunt Lucy's; it was after midnight. As I approached the house, I could hear the sound of music and laughter. I suddenly had a horrible, sinking feeling. As I got nearer, I could see that every light in the house was blazing. Oh no! When I opened the front door, the sound of music was deafening. The house was packed full of people. A number of drinks had been spilled onto the floor, and there were people lying, obviously drunk, on the sofa. The house was a total mess.

"Jill! Glad you made it," Amber said.

"What's going on?"

"We thought we'd have a few people over."

"A few?"

"You don't mind, do you?"

Pearl appeared. "Yeah, you weren't here, so we thought: what harm could it do?"

***

It took me thirty minutes to clear all the guests out; some of them had to be carried by their friends. It then took me another six hours to clean up the place. The twins had offered to help, but they were the wrong side of tipsy to be of any use. And besides, I was so angry, I didn't trust myself not to murder both of them.

By dawn, I was completely shattered. So much for chilling out.

Chapter 25

I slept until early afternoon. I was dreading Aunt Lucy's return because although I'd done my best to clean up, there were a few breakages, and a wine stain on the carpet which I hadn't managed to remove.

Kathy's call caught me on the hop.

"Jill, can you come over straight away to watch the kids? I've lost a filling, and I've been in agony all morning. I've been ringing around for hours, and I've just managed to get an emergency appointment, but if I'm not there in forty minutes, they won't be able to see me."

"Can't Peter do it?"

"He's at work—overtime. I've tried to contact him, but he's not answering his phone. Please, Jill. It's urgent or I wouldn't ask. This tooth is giving me real gyp. Please."

"Yeah, okay. I'm on my way."

I magicked myself over to Washbridge, picked up my car, and drove to Kathy's.

"You're a lifesaver," Kathy said, on her way out of the door.

"Good luck."

"Auntie Jill!" Lizzie said. "Can we go and see the chickens?"

"Err—I'm not sure about that."

"Please," Mikey said. "Can we go and have a look at them?"

"Can't you just look at them through your window?"

"We want to see them properly."

"Does Mummy let you go next door?"

"Oh yes," Lizzie said. "All the time."

"Yes, she does," Mikey said.

Hmm? Was I being played? Maybe, but what harm could it do? And besides, if they were busy looking at the chickens, I wouldn't have to come up with ways to entertain them. That was a plus.

"Okay then. Put your coats on though; it's a bit nippy outside. Are you absolutely sure the neighbours won't mind?"

"Mr and Mrs Flood said we can," Mikey said.

"Just one thing, Mikey," I said. "You'd better leave that drum behind. It might scare the chickens."

"Aw."

"Leave the drum, or no chickens."

"Aw, okay then." He put it on the table.

The kids rushed around to the next door neighbours' house, and I followed. I glanced through their window to see if I could spot either Mr or Mrs Flood, but there was no sign of life. The kids were standing next to an old wooden gate, which had wire mesh tacked to it to keep the chickens in.

"Can we go in?" Mikey said.

"No, you have to stay on this side of the gate. You can see them okay from here."

After a while, one of the chickens came over to the gate; that made the kids scream with laughter. This was going to be a lot easier than I'd thought. I'd never been any good at thinking up games to keep the kids amused. Most of the toys they had were boring, and I certainly didn't want to have to look at Lizzie's horrible beanie creations. The chickens could keep them entertained until Kathy came back. Job done.

My phone rang.

"Mrs V? Is that you, Mrs V?"

The reception was terrible, I could barely hear her, so I started walking down the drive to see if I could get a better signal.

"Mrs V?" It was useless; I couldn't hear a thing.

Then, I heard a clang. The next thing I knew, something small and feathery came rushing past my feet. I turned around and realised that Mikey and Lizzie had opened the gate while I wasn't looking, and one of the chickens had got out. Oh no! I rushed back up the drive.

"Come out, you two. Come out of there now!" I shouted.

"But Auntie—"

"Get out here now!"

The kids came back through the gate, and I slammed it shut.

"What will Mummy say when I tell her you let one of the chickens out?"

"She'll be mad at you," Mikey said. "We're not allowed to come around here."

"What? You said—"

"You said we could," Lizzie said.

"You mustn't tell your mum. Go back home and wait for me there while I try and catch this chicken."

Once the kids were back in their house, I set off after the chicken. I chased it round and round in circles, but it was way too fast. What was I going to do? If Kathy came back, she'd know I'd let the kids go into next door's garden, and then I'd be in deep trouble.

There was only one thing to do. I cast the 'freeze' spell and the chicken stopped dead in its tracks. Ha! Easy! I picked up the chicken statue, and put it back behind the gate. Then I reversed the spell.

Phew! That was a close call.

I was just beginning to think I'd got away with it, when I saw two little faces at the window next door. They looked stunned. Had they seen me 'freeze' the chicken?

A car pulled up. It was Kathy.

"Jill, what are you doing out here?"

"Err—I came out for a bit of fresh air. I was just about to go back inside."

"Are the kids okay?"

"Yes, they're fine. They've been as good as gold. How's your tooth?"

"It's okay now, thanks. But I can't drink anything hot, so I'm going to have a glass of orange. You can have a cup of tea if you like."

The kids came rushing out of the house.

"Mummy, Mummy! Auntie Jill let us go next door to see the chickens."

Kathy gave me a look.

"Err—I thought they were allowed to."

"And Auntie Jill turned the chicken into a statue," Lizzie said.

"She did what?"

"One of them got out and Auntie Jill couldn't catch it, so she turned it into a statue, and put it back in the garden."

I laughed. "Kids? Such imagination."

Once the kids were inside, Kathy turned to me. "What's going on, Jill?"

"Nothing."

"What's this about turning a chicken into a statue?"

"I have no idea what they're talking about. Look, I did

let the kids go next door, but only because I thought they were allowed to. But then the gate came open, and one of the chickens got out. So I sent the kids inside until I'd caught it, and put it back."

"Something strange is going on here. There's something you're not telling me."

"You're over-reacting. I reckon the anaesthetic has affected your brain."

"Why do I get the feeling you're trying to change the subject?"

"What subject? The one where you think I can turn a chicken into a statue?"

"I suppose that does sound a little crazy."

"You think?"

"Come on inside. I'll make you a cup of tea. It's the least I can do."

"Soooo," Kathy said as she handed me my tea. "Who's Drake?"

"Who?"

"Don't come the innocent. Where have you been hiding this one?"

"I barely know him. We've met a few times—that's all."

"Really? Because he gave me the distinct impression that you and he were quite close."

"That's just your overactive imagination."

"In fact, it sounded to me like you were one of the main reasons he wanted a base in Washbridge."

"That's nonsense. He has business here."

"Where does he live anyway?"

"Out of town somewhere."

"How did you meet him?"

"What is this? The third degree? We're acquaintances. That's it—end of story."

"I'm not trying to interrogate you. I just don't understand why you are so scared of the 'S' word."

"Sex?"

"No. 'Serious'. It seems to me that you're scared of committing to a *serious* relationship with anyone, so instead you flirt with half a dozen different men at a time."

"I do not!"

"There's three I know of: Jack, Luther and now Drake. How many more have you got hidden away?"

"None!"

"Even if that's true, don't you think it's time you picked one, and settled down?"

I pretended to check my watch. "Is that the time? I have to get back."

I started towards the door.

"You're running away again, Jill. You have to face the 'S' word sooner or later."

On the drive back to my flat, I couldn't get Kathy's words out of my head. Maybe she was right. Maybe I *was* scared of a serious relationship. Maybe it was time to grow up, and settle down. I had to decide: Jack or Drake. Or Luther. It was time to get serious.

I'd no sooner parked the car than my phone rang. Probably Kathy going to give me more words of wisdom.

"Jill? It's Hilary from Love Spell. I hope you don't mind me contacting you on a Sunday."

"No, that's okay."

"Someone has seen your profile and would like to go on

a date with you. You appear to be a perfect match for one another. I just wanted to check if you were still interested?"

Kathy's speech about the 'S' word played back through my mind. It *was* time to get serious. It *was* time to settle down.

"Jill? Are you still there?"

"Yes, I'm here. Of course I'm interested. Send me his details, would you?"

What? Kathy's argument was all well and good, but she'd forgotten to take into account the 'P' word.

Patience!

Of course I wanted a serious relationship, but I also wanted it to happen naturally, of its own accord. If I was meant to be with Jack, Drake, Luther or anyone else for that matter, then it would happen—eventually—and not because my sister had pressured me into it. Until then, I planned to focus on the 'F' word.

No! Not that! Sheesh, your mind!

'F' for fun.

***

Aunt Lucy was waiting for me outside my flat.

Oh bum!

I'd intended going back to Candlefield to explain what had happened, and to apologise for letting her down. She must have been so angry that she'd come to Washbridge to tear me off a strip.

"Aunt Lucy, I'm really sorry about the house—"

"Don't worry about that, dear. I heard what happened—I know it wasn't your fault."

"Isn't that why you're here?"

"Can we go inside to talk?" Her tone was much more serious than usual.

"Is something wrong?" I asked, as soon as we were inside. "Is it the twins? Or Lester?"

"Nothing like that."

"What is it then? You're starting to scare me."

"I have something to tell you which is bound to come as something of a shock."

"It's not my mother, is it?"

"No, I had to promise not to tell her. In fact, I had to promise not to tell anyone else."

"What is it then? What's happened?"

"Earlier today I received a message—." She took a deep breath. "From your father."

My legs gave way, and I slumped down onto the sofa.

"He wants to see you."

ALSO BY ADELE ABBOTT

The Witch P.I. Mysteries:

Witch Is When... (Books #1 to #12)
Witch Is When It All Began
Witch Is When Life Got Complicated
Witch Is When Everything Went Crazy
Witch Is When Things Fell Apart
Witch Is When The Bubble Burst
Witch Is When The Penny Dropped
Witch Is When The Floodgates Opened
Witch Is When The Hammer Fell
Witch Is When My Heart Broke
Witch Is When I Said Goodbye
Witch Is When Stuff Got Serious
Witch Is When All Was Revealed

Witch Is Why... (Books #13 to #24)
Witch Is Why Time Stood Still
Witch is Why The Laughter Stopped
Witch is Why Another Door Opened
Witch is Why Two Became One
Witch is Why The Moon Disappeared
Witch is Why The Wolf Howled
Witch is Why The Music Stopped
Witch is Why A Pin Dropped
Witch is Why The Owl Returned
Witch is Why The Search Began
Witch is Why Promises Were Broken
Witch is Why It Was Over

The Susan Hall Mysteries:
Whoops! Our New Flatmate Is A Human.
Whoops! All The Money Went Missing.
Whoops! There's A Canary In My Coffee
See web site for availability.

AUTHOR'S WEB SITE
http:www.AdeleAbbott.com

FACEBOOK
http://www.facebook.com/AdeleAbbottAuthor

MAILING LIST
(new release notifications only)
http:/AdeleAbbott.com/adele/new-releases/

Printed in Great Britain
by Amazon